THE EDGE OF DARKNESS

The Edge of Darkness

Written by: A.L. Flagg

Marvel Publishing
Chicopee, MA 01020

This book is a work of fiction. Any references to historical events, real people or real places are used fictitiously. Other names, characters, places, and events are products of the author's imagination, and any resemblance to actual events, places, or persons, living or dead, is entirely coincidental.

Copyright © 2022 by A.L. Flagg

All rights reserved. No part of this book may be reproduced by any means without the prior written consent of the publisher, other than brief quotes for reviews.

Print Edition ISBN: 979-8831919264

This book is dedicated to my *Aunt Darcie*.

You introduced me to this love of the paranormal, and I'll be forever blessed for it. When it comes to witches and magic, you're my number one.

This is for you.

1. SUMMER

The weather was beautiful in Seattle, Washington after a week of gray skies and beating rain. Jasmine Beach was packed with tourists, families, teenagers soaking up the sun before school started up again, and children splashing in the water. Screams and yells could be heard from the nearby waterslide, and the smells of hot dogs and hamburgers filled the air.

Dahlia Mercer sat along a large rock wall at the end of the beach. Her tan and black German Shepherd Clark sat beside her; her arm was draped around him. The waves crashed upon the rocks as Dahlia stared out at sea. Summer was almost over, and Dahlia hadn't accomplished much at all.

With all the rain there was very little to do except work and help her mother around the house.

I'm hungry. Clark's words sang in his owner's ears.

"We're leaving soon, boy. I promise," Dahlia said and scratched his head. He nudged her with full force.

You said that already.

"I did? Let's go, then." Dahlia stood up and Clark followed her off the rock wall. Clark allowed Dahlia to put his leash on before walking toward the entrance of the beach. She gazed at all of the happy faces and wished she felt the same way.

A sudden state of alert closed in on Dahlia, causing her to turn around and look anxiously. Lately she'd been having those feelings more and more, but Dahlia never came across a person following her. This time it was more unnerving and felt closer than she was used to.

From the moment Dahlia Mercer was born, her classification wasn't "human". She got a taste of her abilities when she was just eight years old and was able to talk to the bird outside her window. Aside from talking to animals, Dahlia discovered that she could rejuvenate dead plant life, and in addition, she was able to heal – not only herself- but other living organisms.

It wasn't until recently that Dahlia ascertained her ability to read one's energy – and not just anyone's- but those with supernatural abilities. It was rare if she came across as individual with similar energy to hers, but when the occasion hit, Dahlia never called that person out. Along with energy sensitivity, Dahlia realized that she could resurrect dead animals as well. Her powers frightened her at times to the point where she felt like an outcast. She even loathes herself for being different, but her unusualness has slowly become normal,

and she knew she had to accept herself for who she is: a witch.

Dahlia kept walking but remained alert. The light breeze whipped her long brown hair around as the chattering around her brought her back to Earth. It took her a moment to realize that the talking was directed to her.

She turned her head to find two girls around her age in bikinis and short jean shorts. They were both blond haired and pretty; the paler blond had deep brown eyes and the dirty blond sported eyes in hazel. They were both around her height and would easily fit in with her circle of friends.

"Hi, we're sorry to bother you, but can you take our picture?" the paler blond asked sweetly with a smile.

"Sure" Dahlia replied. The dirty blond handed her a large cell phone and she posed with her friend. Dahlia snapped a photo and gave the phone back.

"Thanks. Can you tell that we've never been here before?" the pale blond asked as she put the phone her friend handed to her in her beach bag.

Dahlia chuckled and replied with, "Seattle's big so "tourist" didn't really come to mind. You two fit right in."

"Is there anything we should do or see before we go back home? I can't tell you how much of our trip we've spent in the cute little stores around here!"

"Well, there's *definitely* a lot of those." Dahlia laughed. "There's a carnival on the boardwalk not far from here. People come from all over to check it out. It's massive and a lot of fun. When you leave here and head through the city, you'll see signs for the Delphic Boardwalk. You'll be there in no time."

"That sounds awesome! I'm Nina, and this is Lily," the pale blond introduced them.

"I'm Dahlia and this is Clark" Dahlia replied. Clark went to town licking their faces and circled around their feet. The two girls laughed, cooed, and pet him; Clark loved every minute of the attention he was getting.

"You should meet us there, Dahlia. That's if you're not busy later. This is our last day in Seattle, and we want to do something we'll remember" Nina told her.

Dahlia hesitated at this. She didn't know these girls. She only took their picture. They were friendly, but it's the friendly ones you have to be careful with. However, this was identical to the way she met her best friend Ryan, and Dahlia had a great judge of character. She had always had good intuition.

"I have nothing going on tonight, so why not?"

"Great! We'll meet you at the entrance. What time's good for you?" asked Lily.

"How about seven?"

"Perfect," both girls said in unison. Dahlia chuckled and gave Nina her cell phone number before they parted ways.

Do I get to go?

Dahlia looked at Clark. "I think you should keep mom company, boy."

Clark whined, but with the promise of raw chuck steak he cheered right up.

***

Dahlia walked through the front door to the sound of 'Hotel California' blaring from the stereo. The smell of honeydew melon lingered, and Dahlia found her mother hands deep in a large mixing bowl. Eggs, breadcrumbs, cloves of garlic, tomatoes, and hamburger meat meant one thing: meatloaf.

"Hey, Mom."

Diana Mercer looked up from her food preparation and smiled at her only child.

"How was the beach?" Diana asked her.

"Boring."

"This hasn't been the best summer for activities. Why don't you check out the carnival? It's going to be nice out tonight. I'm sure Ryan and Mica would meet you there."

"I'm already going. I met a few girls leaving the beach and they invited me to tag along. I mean, why not, right? I have nothing to do after dinner."

"Enjoy yourself but be careful. What are their names?"

"Nina and Lily. Nina reminds me of Mica a little. They're both nice."

"If you run into problems, you know to call me."

Dahlia studied her mother. Something was up.

"Are you okay?"

"Why wouldn't I be?" Diana asked her daughter.

"Well, I figured that you'd be more alarmed about me going out with tourists I just met" Dahlia answered.

"You didn't say they were tourists."

"I shouldn't have to, Mom. You've been acting odd lately. You're definitely not in your element. What's going on?"

Diana sighed and removed the hamburger mixture from the bowl. As she shaped it into a loaf, she said, "I have things on my mind, that's all."

"Like what?" Dahlia pressed.

"Nothing you should worry about. You should go out and have some fun at the carnival. I trust your judgment about people and you're fully capable of taking care of yourself. Should I worry?"

"No, but-"

"Okay then" Diana interrupted and placed the hamburger loaf in a shallow pan. Dahlia sighed and walked out of the kitchen with Clark on her heels.

"She's acting weird, right?" Dahlia asked her pet.

Everyone's weird to me.

"Fair enough."

As they ascended the staircase, Dahlia stopped and looked at a picture of her and Diana taken a month ago. She didn't see much of her mother in her. Diana's eyes were a beautiful shade of brown, whereas Dahlia's were a startling icicle blue. Diana's hair was ash blond and spiral curls, and Dahlia's was brown and slightly wavy. They had their height in common, but they couldn't be more different individuals. Dahlia wished she could be more like her mom, but she didn't know where to start.

2. RESURGENCE

After a quiet dinner, Dahlia took a shower to unwind. She decided on a pair of faded jeans and a black v-neck long sleeve shirt to wear with a pair of black flip flops. She put her hair back in a ponytail and applied a little eyeliner to her bottom lid and mascara to accentuate her long eyelashes. She brushed her teeth, applied clear gloss to her lips, and sprayed honeysuckle body spray on herself.

She went downstairs and heard dishes clanking from the kitchen. Dahlia walked up behind Diana and wrapped her arms around her mother's torso.

"I didn't mean to upset you earlier, Mom."

Diana's hand patted Dahlia's. "You didn't. I don't want you to think that I don't worry about you, Dee, because I do. When you're not in my bird's eye view, I wonder where you are, who you're with, if you're okay, the list goes on. I trust you to make the right decisions. If I keep you too close, you'll never learn to fly."

"What if I'm too afraid I'll fall?"

Diana turned to face her daughter. "Know you have the strength to pick yourself back up and that you're never alone. Someone will always catch you, Dahlia, even when you think no one's there. There's *always* someone there. I struggled with that for years."

"That's why I have you, Mom. We'll catch each other." Dahlia kissed her mother's cheek. "I'm not sure when I'll be home. If it'll be too late, I'll call."

"Enjoy yourself. I'll most likely be asleep when you get home."

"Okay."

"Have fun, kid." Diana continued with the dishes and Dahlia exited the room.

Dahlia parked her mom's SUV near the Delphic Boardwalk, and she made her way to the carnival entrance. She spotted Nina and Lily waiting for her and they waved when they saw her. Dahlia could smell fried dough and she was fully prepared to pig out.

"Have you eaten, Dahlia?" Nina asked as all three girls entered the carnival. She was dressed in a cute light pink summer dress that Dahlia envied, and Lily sported black capris, a light blue tank top, and a black zip up.

"Trust me, I have an appetite for carnival food." Dahlia laughed.

"Perfect! We're starving!"

"What are you hungry for? This place has everything."

Nina yelled pizza at the same time Lily yelled burger. Dahlia smiled. Even after her mother's meatloaf, Dahlia could go for a burger and fries. The food is why she and her friends went to the summer carnival.

"Follow me."

Dahlia led the girls through crowds of people until she saw their destination. The three of them bee lined for the concession stand and looked over the menu as they waited. The smells were mouthwatering.

"Is the one-pound meatball for real?" Lily asked with wide eyes.

"Oh yeah. It's delicious and smothered with marinara and mozzarella."

"That's a big ball."

Both girls laughed while Nina placed her order for a large combination pizza slice and a side of fries.

"Go ahead and order, ladies. It's on me" Nina told them.

"I'll pay for my own" Dahlia replied.

"I insist!"

"No way."

"You won't win, Dahlia," Lily said with a giggle. She went ahead and ordered a cheeseburger and fries.

"I can't let you pay, Nina" Dahlia argued.

"Buy me ice cream later then. You don't want to back up the line, do you?"

Dahlia sighed and ordered a bacon cheeseburger and fries and they all stood off to the side to wait for their food.

As Dahlia scoped for a table to sit at, she noticed a brown-haired stranger looking at her from a picnic table less than thirty feet away. He was surrounded by a group of guys, but he didn't seem to notice them.

"Nice," said Lily, which caused Dahlia to jump.

"Huh?"

"Your eye candy." Lily handed her a burger basket and a bottled water.

The three girls sat down and dug in. Dahlia occasionally looked in the stranger's direction as Nina and Lily engaged themselves in conversation. She was on the fence of being creeped out and flattered by the way he was looking at her.

Once the three girls finished eating, they began their walk around. As they chatted about where Nina and Lily lived, they looked at some of the vendors and even checked out a couple of rides. Because Diana was on Dahlia's mind, all she wanted to do was eat. She knew her mother, though, and Diana wouldn't tell her what was going on with her. The more food Dahlia shoveled in her mouth, the better she felt.

Dahlia kept noticing the stranger wherever she went. As beautiful as he was, she was starting to become slightly unnerved. As much as she tried not to look, Dahlia couldn't help herself.

As Nina and Lily waited in line for the haunted house, Dahlia sat on the sidelines with a large strawberry dipped in white chocolate and raspberry drizzle. It wasn't that she didn't want to go through the haunted house, she just always went through it with Ryan, and every year the haunted house was different. She didn't want that tradition to end.

THE EDGE OF DARKNESS   A.L. FLAGG

Dahlia suddenly went stiff. A distinct voice could be heard amongst the laughter and screeching around her. She knew that it wasn't a human voice.

Once Nina and Lily were in the haunted house, Dahlia got up and began to follow the pained voice. She moved through the sea of people until the voice veered her off toward the rear of a concession tent. The area was free of carnivals goers and Dahlia spotted the hurt animal by the rear tire of a black Tahoe. She carefully pulled the small cat into her arms; blood matted its white fur and its dark eyes suddenly glassed over. Dahlia frowned and stroked the cat's head.

She placed the dead animal on the ground in front of her and looked around to make sure no one was present. With one hand on the cat's head and the other on the middle of its torso, Dahlia closed her eyes. Her hands began to glow a light purple - faintly a first - but the harder she concentrated, the brighter the color became.

When Dahlia began to tremble, she withdrew her hands from the animal and sat back on her heels. The cat stirred and got to its feet.

Thank you.

"You're welcome."

It ran off and Dahlia smiled. But that smile soon faltered when she felt that eerie feeling that she was being watched. It only took seconds for Dahlia to see the pair of eyes staring her down from across the street.

3. NUMB

Dahlia jumped to her feet and hurried away without looking back. Panic raced through her veins as she picked up her pace.

Dahlia fumbled backward when she nearly ran into someone, but she caught herself before she could fall.

"Are you okay?" a male voice asked her as Dahlia composed herself. She looked in the voice's direction and saw the handsome stranger that was following her. He was even more breathtaking up close. His eyes were a shade lighter than his hair, resembling the color of rich honey.

"I'm fine" Dahlia replied. She hurried through the small crowd that witnessed her bumping into the stranger; she located Nina and Lily and they waved when they saw her.

"Hey! We were looking for- are you okay? You look like you just saw a ghost," said Lily as Dahlia approached them.

"I'm okay. How was the haunted house?"

"Awesome" both girls replied in unison. "You should've joined us."

"That's the one ride I only go on with my best friend. It's kind of a tradition."

"You guys will love it. Our flight leaves early in the morning, so we're going to head out. Thanks for showing us around the carnival! We had a blast! I have your number, so I'll keep in touch" Nina told Dahlia and she hugged her.

"I can't imagine how long it takes to get back to the east coast" Dahlia chuckled.

"Two stops before home sucks, especially if there are delays," said Lily and she hugged Dahlia as well.

As they walked away, Dahlia could hear them mention popcorn. Food didn't sound so bad right about now.

With nerves as jumpy as hers, she could shovel down three one-pound meatballs.

Dahlia located the nearest ice cream stand and waited in the long line.

"I'm not convinced that you're all right," came a voice from behind Dahlia. She turned around quickly and saw the handsome stranger.

"Why are you following me?" Dahlia asked defensively. She narrowed her eyes at him and crossed her arms.

"I'm observing" he answered.

"Seems more like stalking to me. Every time I turn around, there you are."

"I follow my friends" he replied.

"Oh yeah?" Dahlia looked around. "Where are they?"

The stranger looked around as well. "Okay, so I'm not attached to their hip. You nearly knocked me on my ass earlier and you looked terrified. You still do by the way, so sue me if I want to make sure you're okay."

"I told you I was fine."

"You're a bad liar," he said matter-of-factly.

"Gee, thanks." Dahlia rolled her eyes and turned around.

"Seriously, though, are you okay?"

Dahlia took a deep breath. He sounded concerned, but that didn't mean that he necessarily was. Dahlia turned around anyway.

"I'm okay." She gave him a smile, but by the look on his face, he didn't buy it.

"If you say so. You just seem a bit jumpy."

"I have a stranger following me around a carnival. I've seen those movies."

He laughed. His smile was faultless, and Dahlia found herself smiling back. She couldn't help staring at the curves of his lips.

"At least I got a smile out of you. I'm Ronan."

"I'm Dahlia."

"You're next in line."

Dahlia turned around and stepped up to the window. She ordered her soft serve vanilla ice cream with strawberries, whipped cream, and chopped peanuts. After she paid for her dessert, she stepped aside to let Ronan order. She was handed her large dish of ice cream and Dahlia found an empty table to sit at. She dug in and heard her cell phone go off.

Dahlia took her cell phone out of her bag and read the message from an unknown number.

Hi! It's Nina! Thanks again for tonight! Save my number! :)

Dahlia smiled and saved Nina's number to her phone. She sent her a quick response and slipped the phone back in her bag.

"You mind if I join you?" Ronan stood next to Dahlia, and she caught the scents of vanilla and birch, an odd combination in her opinion.

"Why not."

"Kind of you" he chuckled and sat down. Dahlia looked at the mountain of toppings in Ronan's dish and she laughed.

"What did I miss?" Ronan asked her with a grin.

"I think you're missing the ice cream in that sundae."

"It's here somewhere." He started to spoon through the toppings and dipped his dish so Dahlia could see the chocolate ice cream underneath. "See."

"My mistake. It looks like you raided a candy store."

"Hey, I know what I like."

"What else do you like, Ronan?"

"Black and white horror films, ice cream with the works, the woods, walking around aimlessly, going to drive-ins, brunettes..." he trailed off.

"Very funny. That was lame."

"Yeah, it was pretty lame" he replied with that faultless smile. Dahlia chuckled.

"You like some good things, though."

"What about you?" Ronan asked her.

"Animals, drawing, painting, fairy tales, running with my dog, being outside, and the rain."

"All great things."

Ronan and Dahlia continued to talk and eat their ice cream. Dahlia's uneasiness was subsiding the more they conversed with one another. She found herself smiling more than she thought possible.

"Can I ask you something? If it weirds you out, I apologize." Dahlia was starting to rethink the unusual question she wanted to ask him.

"Go ahead. It's difficult to weird me out, trust me."

"Tell me why I believe that." Dahlia laughed.

Ronan circled his face with his pointer finger and said, "I have an honest face."

"That must be it." Dahlia rolled her eyes and gave him a playful grin.

"Do you ever...get the feeling that you're-"

"Ro! Come on, dude! Party at Mike's!"

Dahlia turned her head and saw Ronan's posse of friends waving him over. She looked back at Ronan.

"That's your cue to go, as well as mine," said Dahlia as she stood up.

"What's your question first?" he asked as he got up. Ronan grabbed Dahlia's empty ice cream dish and placed his inside it.

"Eh, forget it. It was nice meeting you, Ronan." Dahlia smiled and turned on her heel with her purse in hand. She was pulled back and face-to-face with gorgeous honey eyes.

"Try me."

She hesitated at first, but something in those eyes of his were hypnotic.

"Do you ever feel like you're being watched?"

"In a stalker sort of way?"

Dahlia nodded. "The hairs on the back of your neck stand up and all you want to do is run, but you can't because you're too scared to move."

"Is that how you feel?" Ronan questioned her.

"Not at the moment" she replied.

Ronan's expression was sympathetic. "I wouldn't worry, Dahlia. Just breathe and tell yourself that there's nothing there in the dark that's not there in the light."

"Is that what you do?"

Ronan smiled. "Every time. It was nice to meet you, too. Hopefully we'll run into each other again."

Dahlia smiled back. "I hope so, too. I didn't creep you out by that question, did I?"

"Nothing about you creeps me out." He winked and walked toward his friends.

She would've stayed all night and talked to Ronan. He took her mind off of her fear and her mother. It had been a while since she sat and talked with a guy who wasn't Ryan. Ryan was her best friend since she was little, so talking to him was like talking to her mom.

As she walked away, Dahlia had the urge to look back, but she didn't. Should she care if Ronan watched her walk away? Dahlia smiled because she did, and yet, she didn't look back to confirm if he was or not.

Dahlia reached the entrance to the carnival and stopped to fish out her car keys. A slight warmness on the back of her neck caused the hairs to stand up. She straightened her posture and turned around slowly to reveal that no one was there.

She hurried to find her keys and continued quickly to her vehicle. As she approached her car, she stopped in her tracks. Under the windshield, Dahlia could see something being held down by the left windshield wiper, She approached the car, grabbed the folded piece of paper, and opened it.

I've got my eyes on you.

Dahlia crumbled up the paper and jammed it into her bag. She unlocked the driver's side door and shut herself inside. The text message alert on her phone caused her to jump and yell out loud. She checked her phone and found a message from Ryan inviting her to the carnival. Dahlia's nerves were so shot that she nicely declined Ryan's invitation with a promise that she'd go tomorrow, started the car, and took off for home.

4. BURNED

Dahlia entered the house and closed the door behind her. She locked the deadbolt and stared into the darkened living room. She could hear nails on the hardwood floor and saw Clark round the corner by the staircase.

"Hey, buddy. Where's mom? Sleeping?" Dahlia asked as she pet Clark's head.

In her room.

"Thanks."

Dahlia and Clark climbed the stairs; she peeked into her mom's room and saw Diana glued to her laptop. Dahlia had a good idea that Diana was working; she usually does if she can't sleep...or if she's worried.

"I know you're lurking outside my door, Dee. Come in."

Dahlia entered her mother's room and smiled at her.

"How was it?"

"It was fun. I ate a lot" Dahlia chuckled.

"That's the best part of a carnival!" Diana laughed.

"The girls were really nice. I'd hang out with them again if they weren't leaving in the morning. Oh, and I met a guy that didn't disgust me." Dahlia sat down on Diana's bed and Clark rested his head on her lap.

"Really? Was he cute?"

Dahlia smirked. "Cute isn't the word. Tall, dirty blond, eyes almost the same color as his hair, amazing build, nice deep voice, a melting smile, good conversationalist, and did I mention gorgeous?"

Diana smiled. "Does Mr. Gorgeous have a name? A handsome father maybe? Preferably single."

Dahlia laughed. "His name's Ronan. Not sure about the single father, though."

"You got his number, right?"

Dahlia sighed. "No. His friends were calling him to go to this party, so we wrapped it up quickly."

"Maybe he's on Facebook."

"Maybe."

"I'd like to see you date someone, Dee. What about Ryan?"

Dahlia let out a laugh. "Ryan? My *best friend* Ryan? Is that a serious question?"

"What? You two are always together, so forgive me for asking."

"Of course we're always together! We're best friends! Didn't you have someone you always hung out with?"

"Sure. Kristen" Diana answered.

"Yeah, but Aunt Kris told me that you two met when you moved us here to Seattle when I was younger. Wasn't there someone else, maybe in Broken Bay?"

Broken Bay was Diana's childhood hometown, and a place Diana didn't like to talk about. Dahlia wanted to know more about her mother's birthplace, but the subject would always change, or she would be told that she didn't need to know. Kristen didn't know much about Diana's past and Dahlia couldn't get a hold of the one person who *would* know - her grandmother that she never met. Dahlia was at a standstill.

"Of course I had someone in Broken Bay" Diana answered.

"Who? A guy or a girl?"

"It was your father, Dahlia." Diana's mood suddenly changed as it tended to do when Dahlia's father was mentioned.

"Oh. I'm sorry, Mom. I-"

"You didn't know. I think I'm going to call it a night. Can you shut the door on your way out, please?"

"Mom-"

"I'll see you in the morning, Dee" Diana interrupted her daughter. She kissed Dahlia's forehead and Dahlia stood up. When she got to the door, she stopped and turned to her mother.

"I know it's difficult to talk about dad, but there will be a day when you're going to have to tell me about him. I'm not going to stop asking. I think I deserve to know who he was."

Both Dahlia and Clark stepped into the hall and Dahlia closed the door. She walked to her bedroom, and as Clark got comfortable on the bed, Dahlia found clothes to change into. She removed the make-up from her face and grabbed her sketchbook and pencils from the desk.

Are you going to draw me?

Dahlia looked at Clark's goofy expression and grinned.

"Do you know how many times I've drawn you?"

No, but I'm pretty. Clark rolled onto his side as if he were striking a pose.

"You're a goofball." Dahlia sat down on the bed; she plugged her iPod into its large speaker and chose the playlist she usually listened to when she drew or painted.

Can you add me to the picture after?

"Clark! You want to be in every picture I draw!" Dahlia laughed.

But I'm pretty! You tell me so all the time.

"You're right, I do. Your beauty's hard to capture in a drawing, boy."

Clark sat there unmoved by what she said. Dahlia put her pencil to the lean sheet of paper and began to shape a head, Clark watched intently as his owner drew and erased lines.

Who are you drawing?

"I'm drawing someone I met at the carnival tonight" Dahlia answered without taking her eyes off the paper.

Will I get to meet him?

"If I run into him again, yes."

Good.

Dahlia smiled as she worked intently on Ronan's facial features. She wanted them to be absolutely perfect.

* * *

Clark's head perked up, causing Dahlia to jolt slightly.

"Jeez, Clark!" she exclaimed as she began to erase the dark line she made with her pencil when she jumped.

Do you hear that?

Dahlia stopped what she was doing and listened with Clark. Her eyebrows furrowed and she got up off of her bed. She walked to Diana's door and leaned her right ear up against it. She could hear her mom crying as she talked to someone. Who that someone was would be the mystery to solve. Dahlia hadn't heard her mother cry that hard in a long time. She had no idea what she was talking about – Dahlia couldn't understand Diana through her heavy crying. It was heartbreaking.

Dahlia backed away from her mother's door and went back to her room. If she was worried about Diana before, that worry just intensified. Dahlia just hoped that she wasn't the cause of Diana's tears.

***

Wake up! Wake up now!

Clark nudged Dahlia's arms hard with his snout and then his paws. He barked and Dahlia jolted upright. Her bedroom was engulfed in smoke.

Kick the door down!

"Move, Clark!" Dahlia shouted. Dahlia tapped the door handle to see if it was hot. The metal instantly burned her, and she found clothing to cover the knob with in order to open it. She could still feel heat, but it was tolerable.

"Stand next to me, boy." Dahlia stood to the side with Clark beside her and she opened the door. More smoke poured in, and she held her breath as she entered the hall.

Flames surrounded her and Dahlia's eyes began to sting. She tried not to inhale the smoke into her lungs, but there was too much of it. She felt her skin getting hot and knew she had to get out the house fast.

"Mom!" Dahlia shouted into the fire. There was no response and Dahlia looked at the staircase.

"Clark, go out your doggy door!"

I'm not leaving you alone!

"Just go! I'm right behind you, boy! Please!" Dahlia pleaded.

Clark took off down the stairs and Dahlia heard a loud crash and a whimper from her dog.

"Clark!"

She heard another whimper.

"Hang on, boy! I'll be right there!"

Dahlia rushed to her mother's room where the heat intensified.

"Mom! Answer me!" Dahlia shouted. The skin on her legs were burning, and as much as she wanted to kick the door in, Dahlia knew the fire would explode through the threshold. Her eyes burned with tears as she rushed to the staircase.

Before she could start to descend, Dahlia felt the hairs on her arms and neck stand up. She turned around and made out a figure in the smoke.

"What the fu-"

Dahlia was interrupted by a tightening in her chest. She couldn't yell out. She could barely breathe. Dahlia dropped to her knees and her right hand pushed against the skin over her heart. The pain made her wish for death.

Then she heard it. The sound of her own scream.

5. COMING UNDONE

Dahlia groaned. She forced her eyes open and realized that she was just outside her burning house. She looked herself over and saw the burns that stretched over her legs and arms. She rested on her back and began to concentrate on her wounds until the pain was gone.

Dahlia jerked upright. "Clark!" She jumped to her feet and frantically looked around. When she saw Clark emerge from one of the large bushes in front of the house, Dahlia threw her arms around his neck.

My leg hurts.

Dahlia looked at his legs and saw that his rear left leg had been impaled.

"Relax, buddy. You'll be perfect in no time."

Dahlia turned her head when she heard sirens heading in her direction.

"Okay, here we go."

Dahlia placed her hands on Clark's leg; she watched as his gash began to close. Purple illuminated from her fingertips as police cruisers and a fire truck stopped in front of her house.

"Miss, come away from the house!" a policeman shouted.

The glow faded and Clark licked his owner's face in appreciation. Dahlia stared at her burning home and her gaze went to the windows of her mother's bedroom. Fresh tears fell from her eyes.

Dahlia was escorted to one of the police cars and Clark followed behind. He nestled against her legs as she leaned up against the back of the cruiser.

"Is there anyone else in the house?" the cop asked.

"My mom" Dahlia answered in a whisper.

More tears fell as firefighters and police rushed around her and Clark, She looked to her left and saw the crowd of neighbors that gathered across the street. She scanned them and did a double take on one individual. She squinted her eyes and could swear she was looking right at Ronan. No sooner did she look away did he disappear. Dahlia sighed.

"Miss, we want you to go to the hospital to get checked. Do you want me to call anyone for you to meet you at the hospital?"

Dahlia didn't make eye contact. "My Aunt Kristen." She gave the officer her number and another cop took Dahlia to the ambulance.

"Can my dog ride with me?" Dahlia asked.

"I wish I could allow that, but I can arrange for your dog to be picked up by someone" the cop replied. Clark whimpered.

"My best friend will pick him up."

"Here." The young cop handed her his phone. Dahlia took it, flipped it open, and dialed Ryan's number.

"*(Hello?)*...Ry, it's Dee...*(What's wrong? Your voice sounds funny)*...I need you to-...*(You need me to do what?)*...I need you to come and get Clark right now...*(What's going on? What's wrong?)*..."

As Dahlia was going to reply, she watched a gurney being wheeled out of the extinguished house. A black body bag rested on top of the gurney and Dahlia's world went blank.

"Just come get him. I'll call you later." She hung up before she completely lost it. Dahlia bent down to her dog and took his head in her hands.

"Ryan's on his way. I'll see you in a little bit, okay? I promise."

Clark whined. *Okay.*

Dahlia kissed his head and stood up. "Ryan's coming to pick up Clark. I'll go to the hospital."

"Alright, your dog's in good hands."

Dahlia nodded, gave the officer his phone back, and got into the ambulance.

At the hospital, Dahlia was taken to the emergency room and was assigned a room. She was surrounded by nurses taking her vitals and asking her questions. She just wanted to leave, but what she wanted more was to wake up from the nightmare she was having.

Kristen walked into the hospital room. The two women stared at each other until Kristen flung her arms around Dahlia.

"I'm s-so s-sorry" Kristen cried. Dahlia hugged her back and allowed the tears to fall.

"I want to go to your house," Dahlia said.

"We will."

An hour later, Dahlia was sitting on Kristen's couch in Kristen's clothes, wrapped in a blanket. She was waiting for Ryan and Clark.

"I tried to save her, Aunt Kris. I couldn't get in the room," Dahlia whispered through the blurred vision her tears had caused. Kristen immediately consoled her, stroking her hair as Dahlia cried into her shoulder.

"Everything will be okay, honey. Don't worry. I'm here to help you."

Dahlia was jostled awake. She could see Clark beside her, and she nuzzled against his soft fur.

"Dee?"

Dahlia looked up and saw Ryan. He sat down next to her, and Dahlia fell into him. She cried until she fell asleep.

6. EVE

It was just after noon and Eve Gregory was making her afternoon tea of fresh juniper and chamomile. She breathed the scents in and exhaled with a smile.

The telephone rang and Eve picked up the receiver next to her.

"Hello?...*(Mrs. Gregory?)*...Yes?...*(This is Kristen North. I'm a close friend of Diana's)*...I remember her talking about you. Is everything all right? You sound upset...*(I'm sorry, but I couldn't call you last night when it happened. Diana was involved in an accident)*...Accident? What kind of an accident?...*(The house was on fire and I'm...I'm s-so s-sorry...but she didn't...s-she didn't...)*"

Eve closed her eyes as Kristen tried to get the words out. Tears started to roll down her cheeks and she leaned against the counter,

"*(She didn't make it out of the house, Mrs. Gregory)*" Kristen finally choked out. Eve's left hand gripped the counter so she wouldn't collapse.

"And Dahlia? Is she-...*(Dahlia's fine. She's safe and sound at my house)*...I'll cover the expenses for the funeral. I want only the best for my daughter...*(Dahlia isn't in any condition to make the arrangements right now, so I was hoping you could help me?)*...Are you suggesting that I come to Seattle?...*(If you can't, then I'll-)*...I'll come. I'll be there in two days...*(Dahlia would love to meet you)*...I can't wait to meet her. I'll call you when I get to Seattle so we can make the arrangements. Oh, and Kristen?...*(Yes?)*...Thank you for taking my granddaughter in...*(I'd do anything for Diana and Dahlia)*...Thank you. I'll see you soon."

Eve hung up and cried into her hands. Then she composed herself and started to make the necessary preparations for her trip to Washington.

* * *

Dahlia spent her time drawing in Kristen's living room with Clark by her side. She looked through Kristen's photo albums and saw many pictures of her mom she'd never seen before. She found the perfect photograph to replicate of Diana and she wanted to complete it before the funeral.

Thanks to Kristen, Dahlia was given a blank canvas, paints, a variety of brushes, an easel, a new sketchbook, and pencils.

Over the past few days, Dahlia had made statements to the police, had talked to the home insurance agent, and also talked to the life insurance agent. Dahlia didn't want to talk anymore. She was exhausted. She had just lost everything in one night and had no idea how she was going to get it all back. In reality, Dahlia knew she wouldn't.

Kristen returned home with shopping bags in both hands.

"Hey, Dee."

Dahlia tore her eyes away from her canvas and smiled.

"Hey, Aunt Kris. You've been a little busy, huh?"

"Today, yes. I picked up some more clothes for you, so I hope I got the sizes right. I picked up some make-up, the lotion you love, shoes, and necessities."

"You didn't have to do that. I picked up some things yesterday."

"I love to help. I want to get you back on track, Dee. Oh, I spoke with Verizon and your insurance covers your phone, so you can go in and replace it. I think you're due for an upgrade."

"Thank you. How did the arrangements for mom's funeral go?" Dahlia asked. She rinsed her brushes and sat down on the couch next to Clark.

"It went well. The service is in three days. Eve wished you were there today." Kristen placed the bags at Dahlia's feet.

"I wasn't ready for that."

"She knows. She can't wait to meet you."

"The feelings are mutual." Dahlia started pulling pairs of jeans out of one bag. You nailed my size, Aunt Kris."

"Great! If you don't the style of anything I bought, you can exchange them."

"No need! These are awesome!"

Dahlia pulled out different types of shirts, undergarments, make-up, and a new pair of sneakers and flip flops.

"You know me well" Dahlia chuckled.

"I try. Chinese or pizza?"

"Pizza and wings?" Dahlia asked with a hopeful smile.

"Duh."

Kristen went into the kitchen and Dahlia brought her new clothes to her room. She tried everything on before removing the tags; she put the load in the washing machine and walked into the kitchen.

"I forgot to tell you that I spoke with those agents from the home insurance and life insurance companies and everything's all set. Because you're not eighteen yet, your mom put me as her secondary beneficiary on her policies, so I'll deposit those checks into your account," Kristen said as she took plates out of the cupboard.

"Be sure to keep some for yourself."

Kristen locked eyes with Dahlia. "Why would I do that?"

"Look at all the stuff you've bought me and-"

"Stop. That money is yours and I don't want a penny of it. If you haven't noticed, I'm well taken care of. Alimony's a wonderful thing."

They both laughed.

"So, where's the funeral going to be?" Dahlia asked, changing the subject.

"Barrington Gardens. How about a gathering here afterwards? We'll serve chips, dips, raw veggies, fruit, deli platters, and we'll get a nice cake."

"That'll be nice. I want to make something hot. Can I make lasagna?"

"Sure!"

"I'm almost done with mom's portrait for the funeral."

"I can't wait to see it." Kristen smiled.

"It's coming out fantastic. Do you think we can go out tomorrow so I can get a black dress? It slipped my mind yesterday" Dahlia asked.

"I need one, too. We'll have a girl's day."

"I'd like that. I *need* that."

The doorbell rand and Kristen grabbed her wallet.

"I'll be right back with the grub, kid."

Dahlia nodded. She'd give anything for one more girl's day with her mother. She'd give anything for one more day with Diana, period.

* * *

Dahlia checked herself over in the full-length mirror in her bedroom. She had on her new above-the-knee black off the shoulder dress and new black high heels. Her hair was left down and curled at the ends; Dahlia's make-up was simple: light foundation, bronzer alone her cheekbones, black eyeliner along the inside of her bottom lids, and black mascara.

The longer she stared at herself, the harder it was getting for Dahlia to face the people that would be at Diana's funeral. What if she couldn't keep it together? Crying was a normal human response to losing a loved one, but Dahlia wasn't one to break down in front of a crowd. She didn't like crying at all.

She turned away from the mirror and left her room.

Do I get to go?

Dahlia looked at Clark. "No. boy. You have to stay here and watch the house until we come back."

He whimpered.

"I know" she whispered.

Dahlia stood inside one of the Barrington Gardens' four service rooms. It was large and decorated with fresh cut rose bouquets and decor out of the gilded age. The portrait she painted of Diana rested just beside Diana's urn.

"Dahlia?"

Dahlia turned around and saw a woman a few inches shorter than her with shoulder length ash blond hair and brown eyes. She looked identical to her mother.

"Hi, Gram."

They hugged each other and Eve looked at the painting of Diana.

"You did a beautiful job," said Eve.

"How do you know that's my work? I didn't sign it."

"Grandmothers know everything. Also, your mother told me that you're an artist."

Dahlia smiled. "Would you like to take it home with you?"

"I'd love to" Eve answered.

As people entered the room, they all sat down in the chairs before the altar. Kristen sat on the other side of Dahlia while Ryan sat directly behind his best friend.

It was difficult for Dahlia to pay attention to the Pastor and friends of Diana's when they talked about her. She couldn't come to the point of talking about her mom, but Kristen said everything Dahlia was thinking. It was her grandmother's speech, however, that made her tear up. It was a beautiful eulogy, and Dahlia looked forward to getting to know Eve a lot better.

7. SAYING GOODBYE

After the service, everyone gathered at Kristen's house. There was food, beverages, and memories being shared. Dahlia and Ryan opened up a lot of emotions as they shared their stories with everybody. Even Eve had a few stories to share that Dahlia took a fascination to.

By three in the afternoon, the only people left at the house were Dahlia, Kristen, and Eve. As all three helped to clean up, Dahlia was in better spirits than she was earlier that day.

"Why don't you join me for dinner at the hotel I'm staying at?" Eve asked as she dried a platter.

"I'd love to" Dahlia answered.

Eve smiled. "Kristen?"

"You two should have dinner. I have some work to finish up."

"Aunt Kris-"

"You two should get to know each other better. You've waited for this for a long time, Dahlia" Kristen interrupted her.

"Are you sure?"

"Absolutely."

"We'll leave here around five and you'll be back by ten," said Eve.

"Dee, you can use my car. I'm not going anywhere" Kristen offered.

"That might be better, Gram. I can change and meet you at the hotel around five, five-thirty" Dahlia told Eve.

"Perfect. I'll go back and freshen up a bit and I'll see you when you get there." Eve turned to Kristen. "The party was lovely. You did a wonderful job. Both of you did. And thank you for letting me take Diana's ashes back home with me."

"She's your daughter, Mrs. Gregory. Who am I to say no to you? Her will stated that she was to be laid to rest in Broken Bay."

Dahlia remembered the will stating that which she found odd.

"I'll see you in a couple of hours, Dahlia. Kristen, it was a pleasure meeting you."

"Likewise." Eve and Kristen hugged, and Eve turned her attention to Clark. She said a few words to him, kissed his head, and looked at Dahlia.

"I'm at the Sheraton by the boardwalk, room two thirty-eight. I'll see you later."

"Okay."

Dahlia walked her grandmother to her rental car and watched her drive away. She walked back inside, and Clark followed Dahlia to her bedroom. She chose a new pair of jeans, a deep red scoop neck three quarter sleeve shirt, and her heels to wear to dinner. She freshened up her make-up and looked at Clark.

I like her. She's nice.

"I like her, too, boy" Dahlia answered.

* * *

Dahlia arrived at the Sheraton just before five. She took the elevator to the third floor and found her grandmother's room. Dahlia knocked and waited for the door to open. She smiled when she saw Eve.

"Ready to eat?" Dahlia was asked.

"I am."

Dahlia and Eve took the elevator to the first floor; they walked into the hotel restaurant and were seated. They both ordered beverages and started looking over the menu.

"I'm glad we have some more time to talk. There's something I've been wanting to ask you, Dahlia, and it's a very big decision on your part. I know that I've-"

Eve paused when the waitress placed their drinks in front of them.

"Do you need a few minutes to look over the menu?" the waitress asked.

Both Dahlia and Eve said no and ordered their meals. Once the waitress walked away, Dahlia urged her grandmother to continue talking.

"I know that I've been absent from your life, and I would really love to have more time with you. I realize that this meeting was under tragic circumstances. You're my only grandchild, and I know that Seattle is your home, but I'd love for you to come and live with me. You don't have to answer me now. Just think about it."

"Live with you in Broken Bay?" Dahlia asked.

"Yes."

"I'll go." There was no hesitation in Dahlia's voice. Eve's eyes widened.

"You can think about it, honey. I don't want to pressure you."

"You're not, Gram. I want to start over. I want to start fresh. And I've always wondered what Broken Bay was like. Mom never liked to talk about it. I think it'll be good for me" Dahlia answered.

"I agree. Clark is more than welcome to come along."

"I may have him stay with Aunt Kris for a little bit - just until I get settled in. I know he's going to hate me."

"Clark won't hate you. He adores you."

"Do you have any pets?" Dahlia asked.

"I do. I have a large, long haired black cat named Juniper."

"Clark loves cats. He loves everyone. When can I come to Broken Bay?" asked Dahlia, changing the subject.

"I leave tomorrow morning and that's too short of a notice for you, so you can come whenever you're ready."

"I'll let you know." Dahlia smiled.

* * *

Dahlia walked through the front door at a quarter to eight. She had rehearsed how she was going to tell Kristen that she was leaving, and also how she was going to tell Ryan.

It would be the most difficult goodbye she'd have to make, but it was a goodbye she knew she had to make.

"You're back already?" Kristen asked from the couch. Her laptop was open in front of her, and Clark was sprawled out on the hardwood floor.

"Her flight's in the morning. We have to talk about something, Aunt Kris."

"I already know."

Dahlia furrowed her brows. "What do you know?"

"That your grandmother asked you to move in with her."

"How-"

"She told me she was going to ask you, Dee."

"She did?" Dahlia questioned her.

"Yes. What did you decide to do?"

"Go" she answered. Clark's head perked up.

Road trip?

"And you're absolutely sure you want to do that?"

"Yes. There's one thing, though, and it has to do with Clark."

"What about him?" Kristen asked.

"Is there any way he can stay here for a little while? I want to get settled first and I don't think he'd want to travel under the-"

Kristen put her hand up. "I'll tell you what. I'll drive to Broken Bay around Christmas to visit and I'll bring Clark with me. That give you a few months to adjust."

"You'd do that?"

"Of course I'd do that."

Clark whimpered. Dahlia looked at him.

You're leaving me?

It won't be for long, I promise, boy.

Clark got up and walked out of the room.

"He hates me." Dahlia sighed.

"No, he doesn't. Dogs don't understand the situations that we face," said Kristen. Dahlia disagreed silently, and if Clark was in the room, he'd disagree as well.

"I'm going to bed. I still have to tell Ryan ."

"*That's* going to be difficult. When do you plan on leaving?"

"In a few weeks or so. I told Gram I'd let her know."

"After you tell her, we'll buy the ticket and get you set up at school there."

"Thanks." Dahlia blew Kristen a kiss and walked to her room. Clark was sprawled out on her bed.

"I know you're upset with me," Dahlia said to him.

I'm disappointed.

"Okay, *Dad*" Dahlia chuckled jokingly.

Why can't I go?"

"Aunt Kris's bringing you over around Christmas to stay for good, so it's not goodbye forever, Clark. I'll draw you a new picture of both of us so you can look at it every day."

Clark's tail began to wag.

"Gram has a cat named Juniper."

A cat! Clark's tail wagged faster.

"So, no sulking, okay? Time will fly by. Plus, I can explore the town and find trails, parks, and beaches for us to walk."

Now you're teasing me.

* * *

Dahlia was dreading this. She stood in front of Ryan's house trying to build up the courage to tell him she was leaving Seattle. They'd been best friends for over a decade and if she could take him with her, she would.

She finally took a few steps and the front door opened.

"What's up, Dee? I was just about to call you" Ryan told her.

"We have to talk."

"About what?"

Dahlia sighed. "You remember my Gram, right?"

"Yeah" Ryan replied.

"Well, she asked me to live with her."

"You're not going, right?"

Dahlia didn't answer him.

"*Right?*" he added.

She looked at him sympathetically.

"Are you serious?! You're going?!" Ryan exclaimed in anger.

"Yes, I'm going. I'm-"

"You don't even know your grandmother and you're moving in with her? Over three thousand miles away?!" he interrupted her.

"Hey, she's my only living blood relative!"

"She's not your only family! You have me and Kris!"

"I know that! I can't live here anymore, Ryan! Everything reminds me of my mom! Do you want me to be unhappy? I sure as hell don't!" Dahlia yelled at him.

"You know I don't want that." His demeanor suddenly changed from angry to collected, but the hurt was still in his eyes.

"I have to do this. I need new memories."

Ryan pulled Dahlia to him and soothed her. He whispered an apology as she calmed her crying.

"I don't want you to go, Dee."

"I know. You can always visit. Aunt Kris is driving over in December, so go with her and spend a few days with me."

"You know I will. Just promise that if you don't like it in Broken Bay, you'll come home."

"Obviously!" Dahlia chuckled.

Dahlia and Ryan spent the day talking and reminiscing. When she started to feel guilty about leaving, Dahlia reminded herself that her decision to move wasn't a bad one. Her mind was made up and no one could make her change it.

* * *

It was the day before Dahlia's trip to Massachusetts. For the last two and a half weeks she was pulled every which way to get prepared to move and to also say goodbye to her friends. Her bags were packed and ready to go, and now she wanted to collect herself.

Dahlia walked along Jasmine Beach until she came across the large mass of rocks she and Clark love to sit on. She'd miss being able to look out over the water from that spot. She'd miss everything.

"I thought that was you," said a voice behind Dahlia. She turned their head and saw Ronan standing on the rocks.

"Hi." Dahlia smiled at him. "No posse today?"

"Not today" he chuckled. "Can I sit with you?"

"Yeah."

Ronan sat down beside Dahlia. He smelled strongly of burning wood.

"Were you camping?" she asked him.

Ronan smiled. "You can smell it?"

"Campfires are potent. I love that smell."

"I tend to spend my summer in the woods."

"I've always liked camping. I usually go with Ryan and his family. Sometimes my mom would come, too."

"I'm sorry about your mom."

She looked at him. "How do you know about my mom?" Dahlia questioned Ronan. She thought back to the night when she thought she saw him in the crowd across the street.

"The news. Someone shot a video of the fire, and you were in front of the house. I didn't have a number to call you at."

"I thought I saw you across the street that night with the neighbors. Maybe I was seeing things."

"When you go through something as tragic as you did, your mind can play tricks on you. So, how *are* you doing?"

Dahlia looked out at the ocean. "I'm taking things one day at a time."

"What about your dad?" Ronan asked her.

"I've never met him. He died when I was a baby. He was a sore subject with my mom. What about your family, Ronan?" Dahlia looked at Ronan again.

"I'm an only child. Both of my parents died years ago, but I have my Aunt Rosalie who's more like my mother than my aunt. I'm twenty-two and she's still here for me just as much as she was when I was younger."

"That's because she loves you" Dahlia replied.

"And I love *her*. She does a lot for me. She keeps me in line and is my voice of reason; my Jiminy Cricket." Ronan laughed and Dahlia smiled. She stayed silent as she looked out at the water. She didn't notice Ronan looking at her.

"What's next, Dahlia?"

Dahlia looked at the beautiful human being next to her. "Move."

Ronan furrowed his brow.

"I mean, I'm moving. I leave tomorrow morning for Massachusetts" Dahlia explained.

"Wow. That's quite a commute" Ronan answered.

"I can't stay here. There will always be a reminder of what happened and all I want is to start over. I need to make good memories and I can't think of a better place than somewhere I've never been to where nobody knows who I am. Maybe I can learn something new about my mom. I kind of..." she trailed off, looking away from him.

"You kind of what?"

"I kind of feel guilty for leaving" Dahlia replied.

"Why?"

"This is my home. I grew up here. I'm leaving my friends and everything that's familiar to me and I'm horrified, Ronan."

"There's nothing wrong with being scared, Dahlia. Fear doesn't need conquering. We face it, but not all fears will be confronted. Don't feel guilty. You do what you have to do to be happy. If that means you have to move across the country, then so be it."

Dahlia smiled. "Thank you."

Ronan smiled back and they watched the waves hit the rocks without a word. She knew he was right. Dahlia was definitely on the edge, but her move to Broken Bay was making her more excited than guilty now. It took a stranger to open her eyes and saying goodbye to Ronan was something she didn't want to do.

That night when she returned home, Dahlia started a new drawing of Ronan.

8. BROKEN BAY

Dahlia woke up with butterflies in her stomach. She had three hours until she would be on a plane to her new home. She hopped in the shower; she blow-dried her hair, applied her make-up, and changed into the outfit she picked out the previous night with her friend Mica.

Kristen was making breakfast when Dahlia entered the kitchen.

"Are you hungry? I made everything you like." Kristen smiled.

"It smells great." Dahlia sat down at the table and Clark sat by her feet. Kristen plated scrambled eggs, three pancakes, bacon, and a bagel with cream cheese, and placed the food in front of Dahlia.

"Now *that's* breakfast" Dahlia chuckled. Kristen laughed and made a plate for herself.

"I have something for you. Actually, it's from your mother. She had me pick it up for her just before she died." Kristen grabbed a small box from the counter and handed it to Dahlia before sitting down across from her.

"Really?" Dahlia lifted the lid of the box; her eyes widened when a beautiful white gold ring was exposed. The stone matched the color of her eyes, and an intricate array of white gold vines secured the stone to the band.

"This is beautiful."

"I think it was going to be a birthday gift, but I think it makes a perfect going away present if you ask me," said Kristen.

"Thank you" Dahlia told her. She placed the ring on her right ring finger and watched the aquamarine stone sparkle in the light.

Ryan met Dahlia and Kristen at the airport. They waited with her until a half hour before her departure. It was a teary goodbye. Dahlia had a tough time letting go of them.

Dahlia showed her ticket to the woman at the counter and then sat down. She took her sketchbook out of her carry-on and worked on her drawing of Ronan. It was a little difficult to concentrate. Dahlia felt that everyone was observing her and the drawing. What if someone knew Ronan? Then again, she was leaving Washington for good, so why should she care?

She put the sketchbook away and waited until her flight was called to board.

Dahlia found her seat on the plane and placed her carry-on in the overhead storage compartment. She sat down and buckled her seat belt; she had never been this nervous to fly. Then again, the last time she was on a plane, she was with Diana, and Dahlia's ticket wasn't a one-way flight.

It wasn't until she was in the air did that paranoid feeling of being intensely watched hit her. Dahlia looked around and saw that no one was paying her any mind. Of course, they wouldn't when she was looking for them. She leaned back against her seat and looked out at the open blue sky through the window.

* * *

After a change-over in Atlanta, Dahlia finally arrived at Logan International Airport, She grabbed her carry-on and proceeded off the airplane. When she stepped into the terminal, Dahlia spotted and Eve and smiled. They embraced each other and then started toward the baggage claim.

"I'm so glad you're here. I've been working on your room, and I think you'll like it" Eve told her granddaughter.

"I'm sure I will! I'm happy to be here."

Dahlia and Eve grabbed Dahlia's suitcases and Dahlia followed her grandmother through the airport.

"How was your flight?" Eve asked as they walked through the parking lot.

"I slept through most of it, but it was good."

"Good."

They approached a black Jeep Cherokee and Eve unlocked the vehicle. The suitcases were placed in the backseat and Dahlia got comfortable in the passenger's seat. Eve started the car and backed out of her parking spot.

"Are you ready to see your new house?"

Dahlia smiled and looked at Eve. "Absolutely."

Dahlia didn't pay much attention to where she was going as her grandmother drove along the east coast.

When Dahlia saw the 'You're Now Entering Broken Bay' sign, she took a deep breath and an unusual calm eased through her. She couldn't understand the feeling.

"Welcome home, Dahlia" Eve told her. Dahlia grinned and continued to look at everything as they drove by.

"I'm driving straight to the house. A friend of mine's going to show you around town in a little bit" Eve added.

"Wait, *you're* not showing me around Broken Bay?" Dahlia questioned.

"I have to go to the shop for a little while."

"Shop?"

"I own a business in town. I sell flowers, herbs, teas, oils, and books." Eve took a right on Old Salem Hill.

"That's awesome! What's it called?"

"Eve's Botanicals."

"Love it."

"If you ever want a job, I'll find something for you to do."

"Thanks, Gram."

"The house is just up ahead on the left."

Dahlia kept her eyes on the left-hand side of the side. Less than a minute later, a large old Victorian appeared. Eve pulled into the driveway and parked in front of the garage one hundred feet from the road.

"Holy crap" Dahlia whispered. Eve chuckled and urged her granddaughter out of the car.

9. SANCTUARY

Eve and Dahlia grabbed her luggage from the backseat and Dahlia followed her grandmother to the front door.

"This place is *huge*!" Dahlia exclaimed.

Eve unlocked the door. "Come in, I'll show you around."

Dahlia walked into a large parlor that was decorated similar to the room Diana's service was in. It was like a scene out of *Downton Abbey*. Beautiful nineteenth century decor was displayed, including two dark cherry oak chairs with deep red cushions. It was a room that didn't seem to be used but was well taken care of.

"Just leave your suitcases by the stairs. We'll start the tour down here," said Eve.

Dahlia placed her bags down and Eve started with the room they were standing in. As Dahlia suspected, the room wasn't used. It was decoration, and it was the only room in the house that wasn't remodeled.

Eve and Dahlia proceeded down the hall. Dahlia was shown the half bath before they entered the kitchen. The kitchen was big enough to cook for a hundred people. The walls were painted a soft white color and were decorated with black and white landscape photographs. Grape vines served as the room's border.

Through a large brick doorway, Dahlia was shown the den. It was a very comfortable living area with large plush furniture, a flat screen television, bookcases filled with movies and manuscripts, and a large cat tower. A big fluffy black cat with bright green eyes was perched on a platform.

"This is Juniper," said Eve. She scratched behind the cat's ears and Juniper started to purr.

"Hi, Juniper."

Did you bring the dog?

Clark didn't come. He'll come in December.

Juniper meowed. *You can pet me. I'll let you.*

Dahlia didn't hesitate to do so.

Juniper followed Dahlia and Eve through each room upstairs. The only remaining room was Dahlia's. It was bigger than her old bedroom. The walls were a faint lavender color, and the furniture was made of light oak. Her queen-sized bed rested against the left wall between two large windows. In the right corner of the room, Dahlia saw a large desk with a table easel that rested on the far-right hand corner. Art supplies covered the area on the right side of the desk, while on the left sat a brand-new laptop and laptop bundle still in its packaging. Dahlia squealed.

"Kristen bought you the laptop and its accessories and had them sent here to the house. I didn't put anything on the walls because I thought you might like to frame and display your own work" Eve told Dahlia.

"Thank you! This room's awesome! I'll have to thank Aunt Kris for the computer. I had no idea she was going to do that." Dahlia hugged her grandmother.

"I went shopping for you and got some clothes along with the art supplies. I did have some help with the sizes from Kristen and more help picking out the clothes from the person who's showing you around Broken Bay." Eve walked over to the closet and opened it to expose new clothing hanging up and a few bags on the floor.

"You didn't have to do that," Dahlia said as she skimmed through the jeans and tops on hangers.

"I wanted to, honey. There's one more thing I want to show you before you unpack."

"Okay."

Dahlia followed Eve downstairs, through the kitchen, and out a door to the back deck. Dahlia spotted a rather large greenhouse in the middle of the backyard, and they made their way toward it. Juniper walked beside them.

They entered the greenhouse and Dahlia was overwhelmed by the mixture of scents by the herbs and flowers her grandmother was growing.

"I could live in here," Dahlia said as she inhaled deeply.

"I also have a garden outside during the summer, but I moved the plants in here last week."

"Do you grow fruits and vegetables, too?" Dahlia asked with hope in her eyes.

"I grow strawberries, raspberries, blueberries, cherry tomatoes, beefsteak tomatoes, cucumbers, sweet peppers, pumpkins, watermelon, romaine lettuce, and string beans."

"Sounds like a great salad" Dahlia chuckled.

She smiled. "My house is your sanctuary, Dahlia. Whatever you're afraid of out there, you don't have to be afraid of in here."

Dahlia nodded. She was unsure of what Eve was getting at.

"How long have you known?" Eve asked as Dahlia smelled a nearby rose. She straightened her posture and furrowed her brows.

"How long have I known what?" she questioned.

"That you're a witch, dear."

Dahlia's eyes widened. "How do you-"

"That's quite simple to figure out, Dahlia. You have Xaden blood coursing through your veins, and I, myself, am a witch."

A sense of relief came over Dahlia. She wasn't the only one in her family who was different.

"Xaden blood?"

"Our witch heritage. A source of your power, and a powerful family in the craft."

"What can you do, Gram?"

"Well, I'm known as an Alchemist. I can create elixirs and potions for any ailment. And I can control the elements and manipulate them" Eve replied. Dahlia looked confused.

"Watch" Eve added. She grabbed her watering can and tipped it slowly. Water began to trickle from the spout and with her free hand, Eve made a 'stop' gesture. The water flow halted immediately; Eve's hand loosened and the liquid began to move freely around Dahlia and Juniper in small and medium sized water droplets. Dahlia was in awe at this talent and Juniper attacked the water drops with his teeth and batted at them with his paws.

"Amazing" Dahlia breathed.

"Have you ever tried?" Eve asked as the water returned to the pail.

"No. I'm not sure if I'm capable of that or not" Dahlia replied.

"Try. Concentrate on the water and what you want it to do. Clear your mind of everything and only focus on the water" Eve told her. Dahlia nodded and Eve began to pour the water. Dahlia put her hand out and the liquid raced to her in a large ball. It stopped half an inch from her palm; as Dahlia's hand changed its position right side up, the large ball of water transformed into a heart that floated just inches above her palm.

"I think you're very capable." Eve smiled.

"I guess I am" Dahlia whispered as she stared at the water heart she created before her very eyes.

"If you can control water like this, there's no doubt in my mind that you can control other elements. See that sunflower in the pot there?" Eve asked as she pointed to the small growing sunflower in a bright blue flowerpot.

"Yes."

"Uproot it."

"Huh?"

"Uproot it. Concentrate on taking the sunflower out of the pot."

"I don't think I-"

"Stop doubting yourself and try!"

"Okay! I'll try."

Dahlia stared at the plant and focused on removing it carefully without harming it. When the plant began to move, her focus was lost.

"Oh, my god! I did it!"

"Excellent. We can work on that later. Now, I want you to concentrate on every emotion you've ever experienced and picture fire."

"Fire?" Dahlia questioned. Eve nodded. Dahlia did what was asked of her, but the water heart stayed the same. She concentrated harder, but nothing happened.

"Why am I focusing on fire? Nothing's happening, Gram."

"Those who have the power to control the elements can create witch flame" Eve answered.

"Witch flame?" Dahlia willed the water to go back into the watering can.

"It's ten times hotter than regular fire, although I may be mistaken, and it could be hotter. It's used to destroy magical objects and has been used as a weapon against other supernatural entities. The flame has a window of time before it can't be extinguished. Every woman in my family was able to create it."

"Except me," said Dahlia.

"You just discovered you can control the elements, dear. It takes time. What else can you do?"

"I can talk to animals, heal myself and other living organisms, I can sense someone's energy, and..." Dahlia trailed off.

"And what?" Eve could see that Dahlia didn't want to say it. She saw the fear in her eyes. "You can tell me, honey."

Dahlia took a deep breath. "I can resurrect dead organisms."

Eve smiled.

"What?" Dahlia added.

"You have the same look on your face your mother did when she first told me about her resurrection power. It's nothing to be ashamed of, Dahlia. It's a very rare gift to possess."

"Wait...my mother?" Dahlia blurted out.

"Of course! Where do you think you inherited that ability from?"

Dahlia felt as if all the air was removed from her lungs.

"I never...I never told her" Dahlia whispered as her gaze shifted to the floor. Eve placed her arm around her granddaughter's shoulder.

"Diana already knew, Dahlia. She's known since you were an infant."

Dahlia's eyes began to water.

"Why didn't she tell me?"

"Diana didn't want you to be a part of that world, honey. She knew that you were practicing, and she kept her eye on you. I've been called a few times for advice, but I believed Diana had your best interest at heart. If there was a threat of danger, she would've been there" Eve replied.

Tears fell from Dahlia's eyes. "I tried to save her, but the fire...the flames were too hot, and I couldn't...I thought she'd hate me if she knew the truth! That's why I didn't tell her, Gram!"

Eve held Dahlia as she crumbled. She let her granddaughter cry out her frustration all the while knowing that Dahlia blaming herself and feeling guilty about Diana's death was far from the truth.

Dahlia was unpacking her suitcases when Eve called to her. She knew that Eve's friend would be showing up anytime, so Dahlia grabbed her purse and walked downstairs. She heard two voices chatting from the kitchen.

When Dahlia walked into the room, she recognized her tour guide immediately from Seattle.

"Nina?" Dahlia asked in confusion.

"Hi, Dahlia! It's great to see you again!" Nina exclaimed with a large smile on her face.

"You're from, well, here?" Dahlia questioned her.

Nina and Eve laughed.

"Yes, she is. I admit, I sent Nina and Lily to check on you in Washington," Eve said.

"Why?"

"Diana was worried and she said you were acting a little off, so I sent my spies in."

"She did it out of love, Dahl. Plus, we had fun that night!" Nina smiled.

"We did. I wish mom said something to me about how she was feeling."

"She did say something, but she just said it to me. Now, why don't you two go on and enjoy yourselves" Eve told the girls.

"You'll love Broken Bay, Dahl!" Nina's happiness was contagious.

"I'll meet you outside," Dahlia said to Nina. Nina nodded, said goodbye to Eve, and went outside. Dahlia turned to Eve.

"Why can't I feel your energy, Gram? I've been trying to, but I can't" Dahlia asked her.

"I forgot!" Eve went into the pocket of her pants and pulled out a small pebble.

"What's with the rock?"

"This is iron. Witches can't sense energy when someone is holding iron or if it's on their person." Eve put the piece of iron down. Instantly, Dahlia could sense her. Her energy was the strongest she'd felt so far.

"Amazing" Dahlia whispered.

"I'm going to warn you, though, that around here you're going to experience a lot of energy that you may be unfamiliar with. Don't be alarmed. You're in a new world now, Dahlia. Also, be aware that iron is used to mask energy on purpose like I did with you. Always be on your guard, okay?"

"Yes."

"Okay. Your new friend's waiting. I'll see you later."

"I'll be back in a bit. Oh, and Gram? Can we keep my abilities between us for now?"

"Yes, we can."

"Thank you." Dahlia smiled and left. Juniper rubbed up against Eve - her cue that it was time for him to eat.

10. THE BROTHERS

Nina pulled off of Old Salem Hill and headed for the center of town. Dahlia kept her eyes out the window so she wouldn't miss a thing. She was shown God's Acre Cemetery, Morgan Park which included a skate park, bike and walking trails, picnic areas, Broken Bay High School, Eve's Botanicals which was a cute little shop near Morgan Park, Broken Beach, and finally Nina pulled into a strip mall. It was the only source of shopping in Broken Bay.

"Broken Bay is adorable. It's different being in a place this small, though," said Dahlia as she got out of the car.

"It's small, but not *too* small. Besides, you lived in a huge city, Dahl. You don't mind if I call you that, do you?" Nina asked.

"I don't mind. I'm sure I'll love living here like I loved living in Seattle" Dahlia replied. She followed Nina toward a restaurant called Hugo's.

"This place has great Italian food and is the hot spot where food's concerned. I mean, there's Wendy's and McDonald's, but I'd rather have a real meal" Nina chuckled.

"I agree with you."

Both girls stepped into the restaurant and were seated by the hostess. As Dahlia got settled in her seat, she noticed a tear drop birthmark at the corner of Nina's right eye. It was distinct and faint pink in color.

"I never noticed your birthmark until now," said Dahlia as she opened the menu.

"Really? That's the first thing people notice."

"When I have a lot on my mind, I tend to lose sight of things and get caught in my own thoughts."

"Hey, that happens to the best of us."

They started looking through the menu and was interrupted by the waitress asking what they wanted to drink.

They both ordered sodas and Nina proceeded to order a personal meat lover's pizza with French fries. Dahlia decided on a mushroom and hamburger calzone with a garden salad.

"I'm sorry about your mom. I tried calling you, but the number wasn't in service," Nina said once the waitress walked away.

"Thanks. Everything was destroyed, so I got a new phone. I waited to get it replaced, though. I have the same number, but I'll need your number again."

Nina smiled and took out her cell phone. Within seconds, Dahlia's phone went off.

"Now you have my number. Are you excited about starting school on Monday? It won't take you long to catch up since it's only been two weeks into the school year." Nina put her phone back in her purse.

"I'm more excited that I know someone before I step into the building" Dahlia chuckled.

"Lily can't wait to see you, and you have to meet the guys. You'll fit right in" Nina assured her.

"I'm sure I will. I can't wait to see Lily, either."

"Oh, I hope you like the clothes I picked out for you! I chose what I'd wear."

"You did great! Thanks." Dahlia smiled.

When their food arrived, Nina and Dahlia talked as they ate. Dahlia remembered what her grandmother said about experiencing energies and she couldn't feel anything yet. Was Nina carrying iron so Dahlia couldn't sense her? She knew that she had to relax.

Nina's phone went off and she looked at her text.

"Hey, would you mind if some people joined us?" Nina asked.

Dahlia swallowed the piece of calzone in her mouth before answering with, "I don't mind at all."

Nina grinned and replied to her text message.

"I have a hankering for a hot fudge sundae anyway." Nina laughed.

"I second that" Dahlia replied with a smile to match Nina's.

"We'll wait until they get here and order them. The sundaes are big enough to feed two."

"My type of sundae."

After ten minutes of waiting, the girls decided to order their ice cream.

"If they don't make it in time for dessert, oh well" Nina chuckled. Dahlia laughed. Her attention was suddenly taken; a tall, good-looking boy around her age entered the restaurant. The other individual who entered with him, Dahlia was certain, had to be his brother or a relative of some sort. She tore her eyes away before he noticed. She felt even more embarrassed when the two boys stopped beside the table. Dahlias body began to stiffen, but she tried her hardest to mask it. A familiar energy like her grandmother's consumed her entirely and it was coming from both of the boys.

When the one standing next to her side of the table looked at her with concern, she smiled and relaxed her nerves the best she could. Was she that transparent?

Nina stood right up and hugged the one closest to her. They sat down and Dahlia made room for the other guy to sit.

"Dahlia, this is Reid Wesley and that's Carter sitting next to you. Guys, meet Dahlia Mercer" Nina introduced them.

"It's nice to meet you," said Carter. His eyes were dark green, and his short cut hair was black.

First Ronan, now Carter. Where are these hotties coming from?, Dahlia wondered to herself.

"Likewise."

"Nina's been saying nothing but good things" Reid told Dahlia.

The waitress approached the table with the sundaes and four spoons. Reid had the same color hair and eyes as Carter, except that Reid's hair was a little longer. They both had sharp features, but Carter was stop-you-in-your-tracks handsome.

Nina and Reid dug into their ice cream; Dahlia handed Carter a spoon.

"Help me devour this, would you?" she asked him as she scooped ice cream onto her utensil.

"One bite and you won't want to share" Carter replied as he took the spoon from her hand.

"I can't eat this by myself. Normally, yeah, I could, but I ate a lot before this" Dahlia chuckled. Carter grinned and took a bite of the brownie.

"How long have you two been together?" Dahlia added, looking at Nina and Reid.

"How'd you know?" Nina asked her.

"It's not rocket science, guys" Carter answered. Dahlia laughed.

"We've been together since we were twelve," said Nina.

"They're attached at the hip. It's disgusting." Carter smirked. Reid threw a bunched-up napkin at his brother.

"I wouldn't say it's disgusting, Carter. People would be lucky to have what they have. That's the kind of relationship I'd love to have with someone," Dahlia said to him.

"He wouldn't know, Dahl. Carter hasn't had that love connection, yet" Nina told her. Carter narrowed his eyes at her.

"Neither have I, but the connection's out there. We just have to find it."

"Well said" Carter replied. Dahlia smiled.

The Wesley brothers stuck around for nearly two hours before Nina brought Dahlia home. Dahlia mostly conversed with Carter since Nina and Reid disappeared for a large portion of the time. He was interesting, and Dahlia often found herself wondering what kind of power he possessed. Not that it mattered, though, since every time he smiled Dahlia lost track of what was going on.

Even so, in the back of her mind, Dahlia still thought about Ronan. It was baffling to her how both Ronan and Carter had the same effects on her. She often regretted not getting Ronan's phone number, but like her mother always said - everything happens for a reason.

Dahlia found her grandmother in the den with Juniper watching the Discovery channel. She was wrapped up in a white blanket with a cup of tea beside her. Eve smiled when she saw Dahlia.

"Did you have fun?" Eve asked her.

"I did! She showed me around, we ate at Hugo's, and I met her boyfriend Reid and his brother Carter. Both, by the way, are witches. Their energies are similar to yours."

"You're quite good at reading energy."

"I've only encountered other witches...I think. There was a girl in Seattle I met at a bookstore and her energy was playful and mischievous. I'm not sure what that means exactly, do *you*?"

"I do actually. I knew a few witches with this ability, and I learned quite a lot, but I don't know *every* energy. The one you just described is a fairy. They're tricksters and always playing pranks, but they're creatures of their word. Humans don't have an energy. A ghost's energy is of confusion but they're also peaceful. A demon's energy is cunning and sinister; pure evil. Those are the only ones I can recall."

"Those are more than I know. I tried to research energies online, but I'm not sure how reliable those sources are."

"It's better to learn from another witch." Eve smiled.

"I'm so glad I came, Gram," Dahlia said. She returned the smile.

"So am I. If you have any questions about your powers, don't hesitate to ask."

"Now that you mention it..."

Eve made room for Dahlia to sit next to her.

"Ask me."

Dahlia sat down and Juniper moved onto her lap and began to purr. Dahlia began to pet him.

"Did mom ever ask you about her resurrection ability?"

"She did. What do you want to know, dear?"

"Can you bring back a human? I know I can resurrect animals, heal wounds, and even cure some ailments, but can I bring someone back?"

"Your mother didn't like to talk about resurrection, and I never figured out why, but bringing back a person is very dangerous and could kill the witch performing the ritual."

"So, if you're not strong enough, you'll die."

"Precisely. I think your mother knew that and it terrified her," said Eve.

It scared Dahlia, too.

11. ENMITY

Dahlia spent her weekend unpacking, organizing, and drawing. She decided to draw something for her wall over her bed, so she drew a large self-portrait with Clark and added the Delphic Boardwalk as the background. Dahlia only did some shading in the background and added color to her and Clark to make the photograph pop. She spent hours upon hours perfecting it.

***

On Monday, Dahlia was ready for school early. Eve made her breakfast before going to work, and Dahlia waited for Nina to pick her up. Juniper sat out front with Dahlia as she waited.

Do you like talking to us?

Dahlia looked at Juniper. "It's something I can't turn off, so it's a good thing I like it, huh?"

Are we grumpier than dogs?

"Absolutely" Dahlia chuckled. She scratched behind the cat's ears. "But felines are more independent. Having this ability helps me to learn more about different animals. I really enjoy going to zoos."

If you didn't like talking to animals, you'd have a real problem.

"Exactly."

You look like the type to enjoy zoos.

Dahlia laughed. "Wouldn't you be interested in seeing what a zoo entails?"

No. I hate them.

"Why?"

Too many cat calls.

Dahlia laughed again. "Lame, but cute."

Nina showed up ten minutes later and Dahlia let Juniper back in the house. She got in the car and Nina backed out of the driveway.

"Oh yeah, those clothes look awesome on you," said Nina.

"You have great taste."

"I always stop at Donut Dip before school for c. You coffee and a breakfast sandwich. You don't mind, do you?"

"Not at all! Coffee sounds great."

Nina drove to the Donut Dip near the high school and the girls walked inside. Dahlia ordered a large coffee, light and sweet, and a bagel with cream cheese. Even after the breakfast Eve made her, Dahlia had room for more.

They arrived at a school and Dahlia spotted Lily sitting on top of a car. She waved when Dahlia got out of the car.

"Hi!" Lily yelled and jumped off the vehicle. She hugged Dahlia and Nina handed her a coffee. An energy was apparent with Lily now and it matched Carter and Reid's. Maybe Nina wasn't a witch. If her friends weren't afraid to mask their energies, why should she?

"Hey, Lily. How are you?" Dahlia asked her.

"Good. I'm sorry about your mom."

"Thanks."

"Where's the guys, Lil?" Nina asked, changing the subject.

"Cafeteria. Dahlia should get her schedule first before the bell rings" Lily suggested. Nina agreed and both girls showed Dahlia to the office. Nina and Lily waited in the hall while Dahlia proceeded inside.

Goosebumps rose on Dahlia's skin from the temperature of the air conditioning. She approached the secretary's cluttered desk.

"Hi, I'm new and I was told to come here to get my schedule," Dahlia said to the middle-aged woman behind the desk. Her hair was jet black and pulled into a tight ballerina bun on top of her head. Her large, framed glasses hid her hazel eyes.

"What's your name?" the secretary asked.

"Dahlia Mercer."

"Just give me one second."

Dahlia nodded and watched her disappear into another room. She looked out into the hallway and saw Nina and Lily chatting with yet another handsome boy. He looked like Lily with a short dirty blond fade haircut.

Broken Bay is a hoarder for hotness, Dahlia thought to herself.

"Okay, Miss Mercer, I have your schedule. I also have your locker number and combination, and an agenda book. You write down your homework assignments and use the book as a hall pass as well. There're pages in the back for teachers to sign if you need to use the lavatory, go to the nurse's office, and so on. Any questions?"

Dahlia shook her head no and took the items from the woman in front of her.

"Thank you."

"You're welcome. Have a great first day."

Dahlia smiled and left the office.

"Dahl, this is Trent. He's Lily's brother," said Nina.

"It's nice to meet you. You can tell you're related."

"We get that a lot. I'm more laid back. It's nice to meet you, Dahlia" Trent replied and Lily nudged him. Dahlia smiled. He was also a witch, and both his and Lily's energies together were stronger-much stronger than the Wesley brothers.

"Likewise. Do you know where locker one-oh-one is?" Dahlia asked him.

"Right next to mine" Trent replied.

"Perfect. How about room one eighteen?"

"Anatomy with Faison. That's the science hallway," said Lily.

"Reid, Carter, and Trent here are in that class, so you're golden." Nina smiled.

"Awesome." Dahlia returned the smile and proceeded to tell them the other classes she was placed into. She had no classes with Nina, one with Lily, and another one with Trent. Most of her subjects were advanced.

"I'll meet you for lunch, Dahl. One of us will stick with you, don't worry."

Dahlia laughed when Lily and Nina walked away.

"Nina's the best friend you'll ever have" Trent told her.

"I believe that. They're both great."

"Let's get to class before the bell rings. Faison doesn't tolerate tardiness."

Dahlia followed Trent through two hallways; as they passed other students, Trent introduced Dahlia to people he knew. They were all very welcoming.

They walked down the science hallway and entered one eighteen. Dahlia immediately saw Carter and Reid sitting at one of the elongated black top tables. Dahlia waved when they saw her.

"Come sit with us" Trent invited her.

"Gladly" Dahlia replied with relief and a smile. They walked to the table and Dahlia sat down next to Carter.

"Good morning" Carter greeted her.

"Morning" she replied.

"How was your weekend?"

"It was good. Very settling," Dahlia said. She placed her bag by her feet after removing a pen from it.

"It always takes time in a new town."

"Oddly, though, I already feel at home for only being here a few days."

"I don't find that odd at all. Plus, Nina's good at making people feel welcome, right, Reid?" Carter asked his brother.

"Nina's good at everything, especially that" Reid answered, pausing from the paper he was working on. Dahlia giggled.

"Does she ever get mad? She's always smiling."

"Very rarely."

"Do you like it here better than Seattle?" Trent asked Dahlia.

"Did the girls tell you everything about me?" Dahlia asked, eyeballing all three of them.

"Yeah" they answered in unison. All four of them laughed.

"Well, I've only been here a few days, so I'll let you know later."

They continued to chat until the final bell rang and Mr. Faison began his lesson.

Dahlia sat through AP Calculus with Trent (and found out that they had a lot in common), and AP English with a lot of new faces - one in which was unwelcoming. She made a mental note to ask Nina who the girl was.

Trent walked with Dahlia to the cafeteria, and they waited in the lunch line. Dahlia decided on a ham and cheddar wrap and fries; she was led to the table where Nina, Lily, Carter, and Reid were and sat down.

"How are your classes so far?" Nina asked as she spooned out some yogurt from its container.

"Good. The teachers aren't bad. Mr. Faison's a bit quirky, Ms. Taglia's laid back, but Mrs. Whittier's intense."

"She has her good and bad days."

"There was a girl who was less than welcoming. She kept giving me these nasty looks during class. She has long black hair, dark eyes, and she's tall."

"Does she tend to overdo the make-up a bit and walk like she's high and mighty?" asked Lily.

"Yes!"

"That'd be Kate Basil. She's the Queen Bee, and when I say Bee, I mean Bee as in 'bitch'."

Dahlia laughed.

A wave of laughter rolled through the cafeteria, and everyone looked in its direction. There was a large group of kids surrounding one single individual.

"Speaking of bitch, would that be her over there?" Lily added.

"That would" Dahlia answered.

"She's sexy as hell," said Trent.

"She ain't shit" Lily told her brother with a disgusted look on her face. Carter and Reid burst into laughter.

"Just ignore her, Dahl. She's nothing but trouble," said Nina as she nudged Reid in the side.

After AP History with Lily and Art with unfamiliar faces, Dahlia met up with Nina and Lily in the hallway.

"Do you think you could drive me to Staples so I can grab some supplies for my classes?" Dahlia asked Nina as she carried four textbooks in her arms.

"No problem! We can head over there now" Nina answered.

The three girls walked out to the parking lot where they ran into the boys. They said a quick hello/goodbye before taking off for the plaza.

Nina and Dahlia took their time in the office supply store. Dahlia grabbed notebooks, folders, pencils, pens, and even checked out the little art aisle. She spent more money than she thought she would.

As a last-minute decision, Nina and Dahlia decided to check out some of the stores - including the boutique Nina got Dahlia's clothes in. Dahlia gave into temptation.

Nina dropped Dahlia off around five. Eve wasn't home yet, so Dahlia looked around for something for dinner. She removed a steak from the freezer and placed it under cold running water. She made a quick salad with fresh vegetables from the garden and started cooking two large potatoes.

Once the steak was defrosted, she made a simple marinade for it; Dahlia placed the marinating steak in the refrigerator. Dahlia did her homework for Anatomy and History as the potatoes cooked and started on Calculus when Eve walked into the kitchen.

"Hi, Gram" Dahlia greeted Eve with a smile.

"Hi. Making dinner?"

"Steak, twice-baked baked potato, and salad. I saw some ice cream in the freezer for dessert if you're feeling tempted."

Eve chuckled. Dahlia removed the potatoes from the oven and took out what she needed to finish them.

"How was your first day of school?" Eve asked as she observed Dahlia's cooking skills.

"It was good. I like my teachers and I met Lily's brother. He's awesome and reminds me of Ryan."

Dahlia cut the potatoes in half and scooped the potato out, leaving the skin.

"A lot of homework?"

Dahlia poured a little milk, threw in a few slabs of butter, salt, pepper, and a little cream cheese into the potatoes and began to mash them with a potato masher.

"I wouldn't say *a lot*. I've already finished half of what I need to, but I'll do that after dinner. Do you want to eat outside on the deck? It'll still be light enough to see and it's beautiful out."

"Sounds great. I'll go set the table."

As Eve gathered the plates, silverware, and napkins, Dahlia refilled the potato skins with mashed potatoes and topped them with salt, pepper, and shredded cheddar; she popped them back in the oven. Dahlia preheated the stove top grill for the steak.

Less than twenty minutes later, Dahlia and Eve were eating outside. Many times Dahlia wanted to tell her grandmother about her new friends and that they have abilities, but what if Eve didn't know about their secret? What kind of person would Dahlia be if she outed them?

Dahlia was lying in bed watching T.V.; she had just finished the last of her homework after a hot shower. She'd been texting Ryan back and forth for a few hours, and when he didn't reply to the latest message, she decided to call it a night. Except, Dahlia couldn't stop thinking about Ronan. He'd been on her mind a lot since she last saw him.

Dahlia suddenly sat up and turned on her bedside lamp. She grabbed her sketchbook and continued to work on the drawing of Ronan.

12. OUT OF BREATH

Dahlia was in the kitchen by six thirty in the morning. She was adding some color to her covered Anatomy textbook and drinking a large glass of orange juice.

"Are you sure you don't want breakfast, honey? It's no trouble at all" Eve told her granddaughter.

"I'm sure. Nina and I are going to the Donut Dip for coffee, and I'll grab something there." Dahlia didn't remove her eyes from her work.

"Okay." Eve watched Dahlia as she kept coloring the same spot. "Are you alright?"

"Uh huh."

"Really? You seem distracted" Eve answered.

"I do?" Dahlia questioned.

"You've been coloring in the same area for the last five minutes, dear."

Dahlia immediately stopped coloring and dropped her pen. "I didn't even notice."

"When one's distracted, that's what happens" Eve chuckled.

"It's not that I'm distracted. I'm thinking."

"Oh. Right." Eve grinned. "I have some things to do at the shop before it opens, so I'll see you around six. I want to pick up a few things at the grocery store." Eve kissed Dahlia's head.

"Okay, I'll see you then. Do you want me to make dinner?"

"I'll bring something home. Have a good day at school."

Dahlia smiled and watched her grandmother leave.

"I'm not distracted" she muttered under her breath.

Denial.

Dahlia furrowed her brows and looked down at her feet.

"I'm *not* in denial" she replied.

Juniper jumped up on the counter. *You are.*

"I'm not."

You are.

"I'm...arguing with a cat."

You are. Juniper rubbed up against Dahlia's shoulder. *Humans never win.*

Nina and Dahlia picked up their coffees and breakfast and headed to school.

"You're quiet today, Dahl. What's up?" Nina asked as they walked into Broken Bay High.

"Nothing" Dahlia replied.

"You sure? You look a bit distracted."

"You're the second person to say that to me this morning! I'm just thinking, that's all!"

"Hey, relax! I didn't say it was a bad thing" Nina told her in a defensive tone.

"I'm sorry. I didn't mean to snap at you."

"It's okay. I'll see you at lunch."

Dahlia nodded and walked to her locker. She spotted Trent walking toward her.

"Morning" he greeted with a smile.

"Hey" Dahlia replied and opened her locker.

"How goes it?"

"It goes" she replied with a grin. She put her textbooks in her locker but kept the Anatomy material and closed her locker door.

"Nice cover. You're a hell of an artist."

"Thanks! This is just doodling, though."

"You do bigger and better things, eh?" he asked.

"That sounds so wrong." Dahlia laughed. "But yes, I do bigger and better things." Trent laughed with her, and they started their walk to Anatomy class.

"I draw, but I'm not that great. The best thing I draw is my version of an owl," said Trent.

"You'll have to show me that sometime, buddy."

"I'll show you in class."

Trent and Dahlia entered the classroom and took their seats.

"Morning, guys" Dahlia greeted the boys. She removed her notebook, worksheet, and pen from her bag. She noticed that Trent was already drawing,

"Good morning" Carter replied.

"Dee, you look smart. Can you help me with number ten?" Reid asked charmingly.

"That's an easy one" she chuckled.

"Sure, to an intelligent person. Help me out, please?"

"Don't do it, Dahlia. He can look up the answer in the book" Carter told her as he narrowed his eyes at Reid.

"Stay out of this," said Reid.

"He *did* say please. Number ten is skin."

"Really?" he asked in surprise.

"Really. The skin is the largest organ of the human body."

"Damn."

Dahlia giggled and Trent pushed his paper toward her.

"My owl," he said. Dahlia looked at it.

"That's adorable!" she exclaimed. "I'm keeping this."

It may not have been a very realistic looking owl, but it was perfect for a greeting card.

"Go ahead."

"I'm going to add something to it, though." Dahlia drew a quick tree, so it looked like the owl was perched on a branch.

"Nice touch. Creepy tree."

"It's supposed to be creepy. The owl is subtle, so you want to make him pop" Dahlia answered.

"I don't know anything about art" Trent replied.

"Now you do," said Reid.

Dahlia sat down at her empty little table in English. She took out her homework and placed it at the top left-hand corner of the table. She removed her textbook and a pen from her bag and let her mind wander as she waited for class to start. Ronan was all she could think about - his eyes and how stunningly bright they were, his hair and how good it looked windswept, how his smile made her knees weak, the deep tone of his voice, and how comforting he was to be around. He had every quality to form an obsession over.

The bell rang and Dahlia snapped back to reality. The classroom door shut, and Dahlia turned her head in reflex. Her mouth fell open, and when their eyes met, she turned her head quickly toward the smart board.

I'm seeing things. I'm seeing things, Dahlia thought to herself.

The chair next to her pulled out and she glanced over.

"What are you doing here?" she was asked with a grin plastered across his face. Dahlia didn't reply. She couldn't.

The beautiful boy she's been thinking about was sitting right next to her.

13. RUN IN

"Are you following me?" Dahlia asked Ronan, still in shock that he was in her presence.

Ronan laughed. "Believe it or not, my aunt lives here, and I'm originally from Broken Bay" he answered.

"Small world." Dahlia smiled.

"How are you?"

"I'm doing good, and yourself?" she replied.

"I'm great, thanks."

"Miss Mercer. Mr. Pierce. Am I boring you?" the teacher asked them. They both looked at the front of the room and shook their heads in unison.

"Good. Save your conversation for after class, please" the teacher added.

Dahlia and Ronan looked at each other and smiled once the teacher turned away from them.

Once the bell rang, Dahlia and Ronan walked to the cafeteria together. They got their lunch and Dahlia invited Ronan to sit with her and her friends, but he declined nicely. She decided to join him where he was going to sit instead.

Carter watched from his table as Dahlia got comfortable across from Ronan.

"What the hell?" He looked at Nina. There was fire in his eyes.

"They met in Seattle, Carter. It was out of our hands," said Nina.

"Did you really expect us to pull him aside?" asked Lily.

"Yes" he answered through gritted teeth.

"Well, we're not you. Besides, he was a close friend of Diana's. The closest in fact. You don't think he'd hurt Dahlia, do you?" Nina asked him.

"It doesn't matter. You can't undo what's done."

"If he was going to hurt Dahlia, he would've already" Reid pointed out. Carter glared at him.

"Don't look at me like that, brother. You know it's true. He's just as powerful as we are" Reid added.

"Whose side are you on?" Carter asked him angrily.

"Mine." Reid glared right back.

"Cool it, both of you. If you think she's at risk, Carter, then keep your eye on her," Lily said. "But don't blame us if something goes down. I think you like her and don't want anything or anyone to come between you, if there's anything between you at all."

Carter exhaled loudly through his nose.

"You need to relax, Carter. Do you sense any danger?" asked Reid.

Carter got up and left the cafeteria.

"That would be a no" he added. "He's a piece of work."

"Leave him alone" Nina told her boyfriend.

Once school was out, Dahlia said goodbye to Ronan and left with Nina. As Ronan made his way to his car, he saw Dahlia's new friends staring him down. He knew it'd be inevitable to avoid them, so Ronan detoured to have a chat.

"What's new?" Ronan asked Carter.

"What the hell are you doing?" Carter replied with a scowl.

"Making conversation. You keep staring a hole right through me."

"What he meant was-"

"I know what he meant" Ronan interrupted Lily.

"You're not welcome here, Pierce" Carter told him.

"Oh, really? The last I remember, this is *my* town, Wesley."

Carter snickered and folded his arms.

"I don't hear your friends backing you up. Your little grudge is getting old. Believe it or not, I'm not here to cause problems. I'm here because of Dahlia."

"You stay away from her."

"Or what? Do you have any idea what's going to happen, Carter? Any clue at all? Or are you too fixated on your hatred for me to see the bigger picture? You hate me for the wrong reasons."

"It's your fault that Diana's dead!" Carter spat. Ronan growled at him, but Trent stepped in between them.

"Carter!" Lily shouted at him.

"That's out of line!" yelled Reid.

"Is it?!" Carter snapped, looking at is brother with deadly eyes. Ronan bared his teeth.

"If I was the person you think I am, you would've breathed your last breath just now. This isn't about our feud. I'm doing what Diana asked me to do, and if you were any kind of friend to her, she would've told you what that favor was, wouldn't she? I'm not going away, so get over it." Ronan looked at everyone individually. "It's nice to see you all again. Really. Either you work with me or against me. She needs protection, and she needs us all." Ronan turned and walked away.

"He's not wrong, you know," said Reid.

"Shut the hell up. Don't forget what that asshole did."

Carter continued to watch Ronan with hatred in his eyes. When he was out of sight, Carter took his phone out of his jeans pocket. He punched in a few numbers and waited.

"Eve, it's me. He's returned to Broken Bay." Carter listened for a few seconds before hanging up.

14. PHANTASM

Dahlia walked into the house and entered the kitchen. Before she started on her homework, Dahlia made herself a small fruit salad and fed Juniper.

As she worked on Calculus, Dahlia tutored Trent over the phone at the same time. It didn't take her long to complete all of her homework assignments. She proceeded to prep dinner for her and Eve.

By the time Eve returned home, dinner was ready. Dahlia paused the movie she was watching, plated the meal she made, and sat down at the table.

"This looks great, Dahlia," Eve said as she cut up her pork chop.

"Thank you." Dahlia smiled and took a bite of asparagus.

"You don't look so distracted now. Did you have a good day today?"

"I did."

"Good. Tell me about it."

"Well, someone I met in Seattle just before I came here sits next to me in English."

"Really?"

Dahlia nodded. "I didn't think I'd see him again."

"Him?" Eve questioned.

"Yes, him" Dahlia answered.

"What's his name?"

"Ronan."

Eve nodded. "I know that you'll have boyfriends. I went through that with your mother. Just promise me that you won't try to go out the window, please?"

Dahlia laughed. "Out the window?"

"Your mother was always sneaking out. Just use the front door. You're almost eighteen, so I trust you know right from wrong."

"You don't have to worry about me sneaking out, Gram. Mom sounds like she was a pill" Dahlia chuckled.

"She was a teenager who loved to rebel against me. She had a lot of rules to abide by and I expected a lot of her. Maybe that was the problem."

"Regardless, you gave her rules to keep her safe. I didn't have many, but I've always been afraid of myself. I've been afraid of what I'm capable of. I don't want to lose control and unleash something I can't undo."

"A lot of witches go through that, honey. There's also some that experience that loss of control and like it."

"I want to control it."

"You will, Dahlia. I'll teach you everything I know. I have books you can read, too."

"Thank you. By the way, I won't rebel. If anything, I'll bother you about using the car or ask you more about the craft" Dahlia assured her.

"You can use the car whenever you want. Maybe we should look into getting you one," Eve suggested.

"That idea's crossed my mind. I'll keep my eyes open." Dahlia smiled.

After a lengthy conversation with Kristen and Clark, Dahlia changed and settled into bed. She couldn't stop smiling, and she'd rather go to bed happy than go to bed upset.

As soon as she turned off the light, she turned off the light, she turned the light right back on. Dahlia took out her sketchbook and set her mind on finishing her drawing of Ronan.

Dahlia stood in cream-colored hallway that had pictures of unfamiliar art hanging on the walls. She walked forward and turned left. There was a large, wide wooden staircase with dark green trim and a closet to the left of it.

Dahlia opened up the closet door and moved aside two large boxes. There was a hole in the wall, and she reached in, pulling out a silver key. The end of the key looked like the sliver of the moon. She stared at it until she heard commotion coming from the next room that caused her to jump.

To the right of the staircase, Dahlia could clearly see a large light wooden table with six chairs surrounding it and the colors were red and white. The wallpaper was gold and white and the gold was velvet material and coming out of the wall.

She walked inside and saw a woman in her mid-thirties with glasses, dark brown hair in a tight bun, and she was dressed in a long black shirt and a white sweater. Further back behind the woman, Dahlia could see the living room and a man lying in a recliner. The television was on, but he was asleep.

"Take this tray of food upstairs to the room on the end," the woman said. She was holding a serving tray with a few pieces of fruit in a bowl and a tall glass of water.

"This is it? It's not even a meal," said Dahlia.

"Don't talk back to me! Go!" the woman snapped at her.

Dahlia took the tray and started up the staircase before the woman could throw a punch in her direction. There were quite a few doors on the second floor, but she proceeded to the door at the end like she was supposed to and stood outside it for a minute. She was scared to go in and didn't know what to expect.

Dahlia balanced the tray on one hand while she unlocked the door with the other. She opened the door slowly and walked inside.

It was some sort of bedroom and very drab. The only source light was a tiny lamp on the vanity. She placed the tray down on a small table and her eyes drifted about the room. She heard a creak of the floorboards and froze.

When Dahlia could build up courage, she turned her head to the right and saw a body of a young girl with her back to her.

"Thank you for the food," the girl said lightly.

"You're welcome" Dahlia replied. "Who are you?"

The girl said nothing.

"It's okay" Dahlia whispered. "You can tell me your name. I won't hurt you."

The girl turned around, but her face was hidden by darkness. "I know you won't hurt me." Then the girl's body disappeared. Dahlia's eyebrows furrowed.

"She's coming" was whispered eerily.

"Who is? Who's coming?"

"You need to go, or you'll get in trouble again." The girl sounded desperate.

"Who's coming, though?"

Dahlia was pulled backward, and she saw the door slam in her face. She turned around quickly and saw the woman from downstairs and she had a firm, hurtful grip on her arm.

"I've told you time and time again! You don't converse with the likes of those people! They're the devil's handy work! You never listen to me!"

The woman dragged Dahlia down the stairs and toward the front door.

"Who was that in there? Who's locked in that room?" Dahlia demanded.

"Go outside until dinner's ready! I can't trust you!"

The woman opened the door and pushed Dahlia out of it. She turned around quickly and saw a boy around the age of twelve with dark hair like the woman before the door slammed in her face.

15. HALLOWEEN MASQUERADE

Dahlia opened her eyes to faint sunlight. She had never had a dream like that before. The house wasn't familiar to her. She had no idea where those thoughts could've come from.

Dahlia turned her head to look at the alarm clock. It was almost six thirty in the morning and she threw back her blankets. Dahlia picked out her clothes, took a quick shower, and got ready for the day.

"So, Dahl, I'm on the Halloween dance committee. Do you want to join?" Nina asked as they walked through the parking lot.

"Sure."

"Great! The first meeting's today after school and I'll bring you home later. They'll let you join late. We're deciding on a theme, but I've been working on an idea."

"What's your idea?" Dahlia asked her. The girls entered the school.

"A masquerade. Everyone has to wear some type of Venetian mask" Nina replied.

"Like *The Phantom of the Opera*."

"Yes! What do you think?"

"I love it! Not your typical Halloween dress up. It's more like a casual 1800's ball."

"Exactly. It's something different."

"You have my vote."

Throughout the day, Dahlia thought about what she could offer as ideas for the dance. She wrote down some in her notebook, but one of them really stood out from the rest.

As Dahlia walked to the auditorium, Ronan caught up to her.

"You need a ride home?" he asked her.

"I have a meeting for the Halloween dance right now" Dahlia replied apologetically.

"That's no problem. How about after the meeting?"

"Nina offered me one, but I'm sure she won't mind." Dahlia smiled.

"I'll see you when it's over. I'll be out front" Ronan told her, returning the smile.

"Okay."

Dahlia entered the auditorium and sat down next to Nina.

"Hey, Dahl!"

"Hey. Ronan asked if he could bring me home after the meeting. Is that okay with you if he does?"

"Sure!"

"I didn't want to upset you."

Nina giggled. "Dahl, have you seen me upset?" Nina removed a little memo pad from her bag.

"I haven't, no. Do you *ever* get mad? I admit, I did ask Reid and all he said was rarely."

Nina laughed. "The truth is, I'm very happy. I have a great life, and if anyone or anything threatens what makes me happy, *then* you'll see my mood change. Life's what you make it, Dahl. You're the only one standing in your way. Your actions and decisions will make the way you want to live, the way you want it to be. It's okay to let the bad in with the good."

"What if you let too much bad in?"

"Sometimes that's inevitable, Dahl. The bad, or the negative, helps us to recognize what the good really is. The bad can benefit us in ways we never thought it could."

"I believe that."

The meeting was called to order by the drama teacher, Miss Keenan. Nina's idea for a masquerade was a hit and didn't need a vote. Food and beverages were simple: cakes, pies, donuts, and cupcakes would be displayed, and punch, soda, and water would be available.

"Does anyone have any ideas for decorations?" Miss Keenan asked the group of ten girls. Dahlia looked at the others before raising her hand.

"Yes, Miss Mercer. What's your idea?"

"Well, I love to draw and paint, so I could paint murals for the Gym," Dahlia suggested.

"I like it! What do you have in mind?"

"I thought I could do a haunted forest, a creepy graveyard, a broken-down house with maybe a ghost in the window, and a full moon scene with fog or clouds and a wolf howling."

"That sounds great! Will you have time to do all that?"

"I'll have enough time. I'll stay after school and work on them."

"Perfect. I'll get everything you need by the end of next week so you can start."

"I can't wait."

"What about decorating the rest of the Gym with giant cobwebs, spiders, pumpkins, and hay bales? Maybe some corn stalks, too? We can really make it look like autumn," said Nina. "We can make Dahlia's murals really pop!"

Everyone agreed. Dahlia took out her notebook and a pencil and began to sketch out her murals. She decided to merge the full moon scene with the haunted forest and merge the creepy graveyard with the haunted house. She was excited to get started.

After the dance committee meeting, Dahlia found Ronan sitting in front of the school. He was reading out of a textbook.

"Hey" Dahlia greeted him. Ronan looked at her and smiled.

"How'd it go?' he asked and put his book away.

"Good. I'll be doing a lot of painting." Dahlia laughed. Ronan stood up and they both started to the parking lot.

"What will you be painting?"

"Murals for the Gym."

"Oh yeah? What of?"

"You'll have to wait and see" Dahlia told him with a grin.

"What if I don't go to the dance?" Ronan asked her.

"Why wouldn't you go?" she questioned him. They approached Ronan's black Jeep and he unlocked the passenger door for her.

"Do I hint disappointment in your voice?" Ronan's grin was sly. He opened the door for Dahlia.

"Why would I be disappointed?" she asked as she got in the Jeep.

"Yeah, why would you be?" Ronan chuckled and shut the door. Ronan got in on the driver's side and started the engine.

"Why wouldn't you go?" Dahlia asked again.

"I haven't decided whether I'm going or not yet" Ronan answered.

"You should" she told him.

"Why's that?"

"We're seniors. It's the last time we can go to one of these, and it's something to do. How bad could it be? Plus, you can see my murals" Dahlia chuckled. She wasn't about to tell him that she wanted to be his date.

"We'll see" Ronan replied. He backed out of the parking space.

Ronan pulled onto Dahlia's street when she directed him to.

"What were the odds that we'd meet again," said Dahlia as she looked out the window. She realized she said that out loud and sighed.

"Pretty good I'd say." Ronan grinned.

Dahlia rolled her eyes. "I didn't expect to see you again." Dahlia looked at Ronan and their eyes locked for a brief moment before he re-focused on the road.

"Expect the unexpected, Dahlia."

"I do now" she replied. "My house is up ahead on the left."

Ronan pulled into her driveway; he recognized the other cars that were parked, and his chest tightened.

"Thanks for the ride" Dahlia added.

"Anytime. Looks like a party," Ronan said, referring to the other vehicles.

"I'm about to find out what's going on. You're free to come in, too."

"I'll take a raincheck, but thanks for the invite."

"Sure" Dahlia opened the door and stepped out.

"I'll see you later" he told her. She smiled, gave him a little wave once the vehicle door was shut, and started walking to the front door. Ronan suddenly grew nervous as he stared at Carter Wesley's car.

"You better keep your mouth shut, Wes," he said under his breath before backing out of the driveway.

16. SECRETS UNFOLD

Dahlia walked into the house and heard voices coming from the den. She closed the door quietly and made her way toward the voices. Dahlia peeked her head into the den to see Carter, Trent, Lily, Nina, Reid, and Eve talking. All of their energies together overwhelmed Dahlia a bit.

"We have to tell her, plain and simple," said Trent. Dahlia saw the grin on her grandmother's face and decided to join the circle.

"I have a pretty good idea what you want to tell me, Trent" Dahlia announced as she stepped into the room. "I know that all but one of you have magical capabilities. I can sense your energies. How did you get here so fast, Nina?"

Everyone but Nina looked at Eve with a confused expression.

"I left while you were talking to Ronan outside the school. Reid told me to hurry here, so I did" she answered.

"Did you know that she knew?" Lily asked Eve.

"Of course I knew" Eve answered with a smile.

"Why didn't you-"

"It's not my place to tell you something that was said in confidence between myself and my granddaughter" she interrupted Lily.

"I didn't want Gram to say anything to you. It's something I wanted to tell you when all of you were ready to tell me about yourselves."

Eve chuckled.

"You must've had iron on you in Seattle, right, Lily?" Dahlia added.

"I did. It's always good to carry iron because of the selected few with a gift like yours" Lily answered.

"What about you, Nina? I get no energy from you" Dahlia asked her friend. She sat down on the armrest of the couch next to Trent.

"I have no magical abilities. I'm actually a reincarnation" Nina answered.

"Reincarnation?" Dahlia questioned her. "That really exists?"

"I'm living, breathing proof, Dahl." Nina smiled.

"Interesting. So, how does that work?"

"*I'll* tell you the story" Reid stepped in. "Nina and I met in the early seventeen hundreds-"

"Seventeen fifteen to be exact" Nina interrupted him.

"Right. She was twenty-two and I was thirty. At the time, I was involved with another witch - a very powerful witch. She found out about Nina and me and put a curse on me when I told her it was over" Reid replied.

"A curse?"

"Yes. I would have to watch Nina die over and over again."

Nina laced her fingers with Reid's. "I don't consider it a curse, Dahl. I still get to be with him forever," said Nina.

"It's a curse for me. I can't tell you how many times I've lost her. I die every time."

"But she always comes back to you" Dahlia pointed out. "I understand what you mean, though. It's very painful to watch someone you love slip away from you."

"We've been doing that for many years" Trent remarked.

Dahlia looked at him. "How long have you been alive?"

"Long enough" Lily chuckled.

"I've been here long before Broken Bay was founded - I brought the others here. My birthday is April fifteenth...thirteen forty," Eve said with a smile. Dahlia's eye widened.

"That's...you're over nine hundred years old!" Dahlia exclaimed. Everyone produced a smile.

"I look great for my age, don't I?"

"Are you all immortal or something?"

"We can all die at any time. We all wear amulets - bewitched amulets that Eve gave us - to keep us alive" Carter replied. Everyone took out their amulets and showed them to Dahlia, except Nina.

"You don't have one, either?" Dahlia asked Nina. Then she thought about it. "You don't have powers, sorry."

Nina giggled.

"But, Gram, couldn't you bewitch an amulet for Nina to stay alive even without her having any kind of power?" Dahlia added.

"I tried. The curse is a very strong one, and until that witch ceases to exist, nothing can be done" Eve responded.

"And that bitch will never die, so until she does, I'll continue to suffer," said Reid.

"What have I told you about that?" Nina whispered to him.

"I know. I'm sorry" he replied in the same hushed tone.

"Do the amulets do more or just keep you alive?" Dahlia asked, changing the subject.

"They enhance our abilities," said Trent.

"What can you all do?"

"Well, I can talk to animals, and I'm known as a Tracker. I can track magic back to its summoner" Trent replied.

"I talk to animals, too!" Dahlia exclaimed with a smile. Trent chuckled at her enthusiasm.

"I'm telekinetic and an Empath. I can sense people's emotions, as well as change how others feel" Carter told Dahlia.

"So cool" she whispered. Dahlia saw him grin.

"I'm also telekinetic. I can control, create, and manipulate fire, too," said Reid.

"Just don't show her in the house" Eve told him. Dahlia giggled.

"And I can create and manipulate the weather, as well as manipulate water. I can't create it," Lily said.

"That's still awesome! Everyone's got a different power" Dahlia replied.

"Speaking of power, what else can you do, Dahl?" Nina asked her.

"Besides speaking to animals and energy sensitivity, I can heal myself and other living organisms, I can control the elements like Gram, and I can resurrect like my mom, I've only brought back animals and plants, though."

"Do you know how rare that ability is, Dahlia? Diana was the only witch I knew who could do that and I've been alive since the early sixteen hundreds," said Lily.

"I wish she told me that. I wish she let me in."

"Honey, you have to understand something. Your mother - once she had you - wanted out of this life. She didn't want anything to do with magic, and that's why she never told you the truth about her. Magic wasn't her anymore. All she cared about was you and your welfare" Eve explained.

"If I brought my abilities up to her, would she have turned me away or told me the truth?"

"I don't know, Dahlia. She always knew you were a witch and she had seen you use your magic. I got calls from time to time for advice, but I think that if you were persistent with her, than eventually Diana would've caved. But just because I say that that doesn't mean that that's what she would've done."

Dahlia nodded. "Where can I get an amulet, Gram?"

Eve smiled at the subject change. "You were supposed to inherit your mother's."

"I was?"

Eve nodded. "It was a large, smooth textured stone enclosed in a platinum setting. Malachite was the stone."

Dahlia thought for a minute. "I saw it in her room. It's color was beautiful with the different swirls of green. It was destroyed in the fire."

"We'll figure something out."

"Why Malachite?' Dahlia asked Eve.

"Malachite enhances the healing ability. Your mother was a great healer, and it also came in handy for resurrection as well. All of our amulets enhance our primary power."

"So, what are your stones, then?" Dahlia looked at Lily first.

"Mine's Aquamarine. It helps me to control water and keeps me focused. It helps to let go of emotional issues, too."

"Mine's Pyrite. It resonates with the fire energy, so it helps me to control my ability. It's also known as Fools Gold, and it can generate wealth," said Reid.

"Has it" Dahlia asked him.

"We're not hurting." He smiled.

"Mine's Rainbow Moonstone, but I also associate with Malachite as well. My stone deals with protection mostly. I protect everyone in this room. It cleanses the mind and can ease emotional trauma" Eve told her granddaughter.

"Amber. It aids emotions and allows me to concentrate. It helps to create a more positive outlook on life," said Carter. Trent and Reid both snickered. Carter glared at them.

Dahlia looked at Trent's. "Emerald?"

"Seraphinite."

"As in Seraphim? Angels?"

"You've been reading. Yes, as in angels. I chose this stone for Trent because of his energy and good nature. It links the physical with the ethereal, and is powerful for opening communication with angelic realms, which could aid in tracking magic" Eve chimed in.

"What happens if your amulet's destroyed?" Dahlia asked the group.

"We'll age and eventually die" Reid answered her.

"Would you still have your power?"

"Yes, but the power won't be as strong as they were," said Carter.

"Does every witch get an amulet?"

"No" everyone replied in unison. Dahlia's eyebrows went up.

"It's a tradition in my family, Dahlia. Don't worry, you'll get one" Eve told her kin.

Dahlia's friends didn't hang out much longer after she was finished asking her questions.

"One more thing, Gram," said Dahlia as she stood up from the couch. "How do you destroy an amulet?"

"The only way is by witch flame" Eve told her.

Dahlia nodded. "Thanks."

"I was thinking about making pizza for dinner. Sound good?"

"Sounds great. I'm going to work on some homework upstairs."

"I'll call you down when dinner's ready."

"Okay."

Dahlia walked out of the room, grabbed a soda out of the refrigerator, and headed upstairs with Juniper trailing behind her.

When's your dog coming again?

"December" Dahlia replied.

That's going to be fun.

Dahlia didn't like the sound of that.

"You're going to be nice, Juniper."

The cat snickered. *I'm always nice.*

"That doesn't sound promising."

Juniper didn't reply.

After dinner, a knock on the door surprised both Dahlia and Eve.

"I'll get it," Dahlia said and walked to the door. She opened it and saw Ronan. He smiled.

"What are you doing here?" Dahlia asked him.

"I wanted to apologize about earlier. I should've come in to meet your grandmother at least before I left."

"Oh, it's okay. You can meet her now if you want." Dahlia opened the door wider and looked at her grandmother.

"This is Ronan, a friend from school. Ronan, my grandmother, Eve."

"It's nice to meet you" he told Eve.

"Likewise, Ronan. Any friend of Dahlia's is welcome here" Eve replied.

"Thank you."

"If you'll excuse me. Lock up when you're done, Dahlia."

"I will."

Eve walked away and Dahlia stepped outside.

"Is that the only reason why you stopped by? To meet my Gram?" Dahlia asked.

"I was bored and driving around aimlessly."

Dahlia chuckled. "Right."

"I was. Plus, I was afraid I offended you when I gave you that raincheck," said Ronan.

"No, you didn't offend me. You worry a bit, huh?"

"Must be my sensitive side." Ronan grinned.

"Must be." Dahlia returned the grin.

Just before she could invite him in, he said, "I should get back to the house. I'll see you on Monday, okay?"

"See you then. Thanks for stopping by."

"Expect more visits, Dahlia. Goodnight."

"Goodnight."

Dahlia went inside the house and watched from the window as he drove away. Her stomach was full of butterflies, and she couldn't stop smiling. At the sight of Ronan, Dahlia forgot about everything else - including her recent encounter with Carter.

17. ENVISAGE

Dahlia stood in the cream-colored hallway. Everything looked the same and she had the silver key in her hand. Dahlia climbed the staircase quietly, so the owner of the house didn't hear her.

She walked to the door at the end of the hallway and unlocked it. She walked inside and shut the door behind her cautiously.

"Hello?" Dahlia asked into the darkness where she saw the young girl before. She locked the door.

"You know you're not supposed to be in here," said a meek voice from the shadows.

"What's your name?"

"You know my name" the girl replied.

"I don't," said Dahlia. "You can tell me."

A body stepped into the faint light. She wasn't older than twelve years old with long ash blond hair and deep brown eyes. Her dress was worn and ripped, and she was barefoot. Dahlia's eyes widened.

"Mom?" she whispered in surprise. Tears filled her eyes, and she took a step closer. The look on the young girl's face was of terror and she backed up into the darkness.

"What's wrong?" Dahlia asked her.

"You need to go. Now. Please go" she pleaded.

"Why? What's-" Dahlia suddenly remembered what happened last time: she was pulled out of the room by the owner and forced outside.

"I can help you" Dahlia assured the young girl.

"Just go." It was barely a whisper.

BAM! BAM! BAM!

"Get out of that room right now!" screamed a female voice.

There was no other way out of the room that Dahlia could see.

"Leave her alone!" Dahlia yelled.

"Just wait until I get my hands on you! Open the door or I'll break it down!"

"Then break it down!"

Dahlia was surprised by her own reaction. She held her ground as the banging on the door continued. The wood splintered and the door burst open, exposing a blinding white light.

Dahlia opened her eyes. Juniper was looking right at her and Dahlia glanced over at the clock. She turned off her alarm before it would go off in fifteen minutes.

Who sets their alarm on a weekend?

"I do" Dahlia replied. She pushed Juniper off of her. He groaned.

You make funny noises when you sleep.

Dahlia rolled her eyes as Juniper walked out of the bedroom.

After a quick shower, Dahlia grabbed a notebook and pencil and went downstairs. There was a note on the counter from Eve telling her that she was at the store and wouldn't be home until five or six in the evening. Dahlia had the house to herself.

In the middle of her graveyard sketch for the Halloween dance, Dahlia's phone rang. Nina's name flashed across her screen.

"Hey, Nina…*(Hey, Dahl! What's going on?)*…Planning the murals for the dance. What about you?…*(I'm going to go to the beach with Reid, Lily, Trent, and Carter. Want to come?)*…The beach? It's October…*(We're not going swimming! We make a fire, hang out, talk, throw the football around, and all that jazz)*…That sounds like fun, but I planned to stay home and work on the mural sketches. I'll take a rain check, though…*(Are you sure?)*…Yeah…*(Okay, well, we'll be a Broken Beach if you change your mind)*…Okay, thanks and thanks for the invite…*(Anytime! I'll talk to you later, Dahl)*…Have fun, bye" Dahlia hung up and continued with her sketch.

It was after two when Dahlia began to feel the itch of boredom. Juniper was nowhere in sight, so she started exploring the house. She was hoping to find things that belonged to her mother.

The downstairs rooms have nothing pertaining to Diana, and the basement was fixed up into an apartment with the addition of the laundry room. It was beautifully refurbished with two bedrooms, a bathroom, a kitchen, and a living room. The idea of moving down there in the future flooded her mind.

The second floor didn't have anything of interest to Dahlia. She wouldn't go into her grandmother's room, the other bedrooms were for guests, and there were only a few photographs of Diana along the walls in the hallway when she was in her teens.

Dahlia saw Juniper sitting in front of a closet door and she stopped.

"What's up? You've been M.I.A. all day," Dahlia said to the feline.

You didn't look in here.

Dahlia's eyebrows furrowed. "That's just a closet."

Juniper groaned.

"What?" she added.

Look again. Really look this time.

Juniper moved over and Dahlia stared at the door.

It's not rocket science. Just turn the knob and pull.

"Now I remember why I own a dog." Dahlia opened the closet door and turned on the light.

"Looks like a closet" she told the cat as she peered at clothing hanging in view. Juniper walked inside and disappeared behind the clothes.

Move the clothes aside.

Dahlia slid the hangers to the left and noticed that there was a door.

Viola.

"Is that the attic?" she asked.

Yes.

Before she could take another step, Dahlia heard the doorbell.

"Just when things get interesting" she sighed. Juniper walked out of the closet and Dahlia shut the door. She walked downstairs and looked through the peep hole. Dahlia smiled, unlocked the door, and opened it.

"Hey, Carter."

"Hi." He smiled.

"I thought you went to the beach with the others?"

"I did, but I got bored, and Nina mentioned you were home, so I thought I'd pop over and say hello."

"That was thoughtful. Come on in." Dahlia moved aside and Carter walked in; he closed the door behind him.

Good. Both of you can go in the attic and I don't have to accompany you.

Dahlia rolled her eyes and looked at Juniper.

"Why don't you go lay down?"

Carter looked at the cat. Juniper turned and walked out of the room.

Dahlia looked at Carter and said, "I really miss my dog."

Carter chuckled. "Why didn't you bring him with you?"

"My aunt's bringing him in December. I want to make sure he'll like it here, first" Dahlia answered which wasn't completely untrue. Whoever was in that house the night her mother died tried to hurt - maybe even kill - her. Just like any other pet owner, Dahlia loved Clark too much to risk his life.

"I'm sure he'll have no problem liking this place," said Carter.

"He'll definitely like it here."

"So, what are you up to?"

"Well, I was going to explore the attic. Care to join me?" Dahlia invited him.

"What do you think you'll find up there?" he asked with a smirk.

"That's the whole point of exploring! Come on." Dahlia pulled Carter by the hand up the stairs to the close. She opened the door and walked inside.

"How did you stumble across the attic? I wouldn't have found it if I just opened the door" Carter asked.

Dahlia opened the second door and found the light switch on the right. "That's the beauty of being able to talk to animals. Juniper follows me everywhere, and I'm starting to think that he's watching me versus wanting to be around me because he likes me."

Carter chuckled. "Why do you say that?"

"You're very inquisitive."

"I know. Old habits die hard, you know?"

"Yeah. Well, to answer your question, cats are territorial. I invaded his space, and soon Clark will, too."

Dahlia started to ascend the stairs and Carter followed behind.

At the top of the landing, Dahlia pulled the cord for another light. The attic was full of boxes stacked everywhere and random, large items: an old rocking chair, a baby stroller, a bike from the fifties, and a few bureaus.

"I didn't peg Eve for being a pack rat," said Carter as he looked around.

Dahlia laughed. "I keep forgetting how long Gram's been alive." She started to read the handwriting on boxes. "She must've saved everything throughout the years."

"Well, maybe not *everything*, but anything sentimental. I don't save anything, but Reid saves mementos of him and Nina in every life they've had together."

Dahlia stopped browsing and looked at Carter. It slipped her mind that all of them had been alive for centuries.

"Is it weird that I'm here? I mean, you were friends with my mom. Isn't it awkward?"

"Not at all. This is where you belong, Dahlia."

"Did you hold me when I was a baby?"

Carter raised an eyebrow.

Dahlia chuckled. "I'm sorry, but I have to know."

"I was at the hospital, but I didn't hold you. Lily and Trent held you, and I'm pretty sure if Nina was around, she wouldn't have put you down" Carter replied.

Dahlia laughed. "Awe, Trent." She continued looking at the boxes.

"Are you looking for something specific?"

"I'm hoping Gram has things that used to belong to mom. I lost everything in the fire, so pictures would be nice. Aunt Kris said she sent me a bunch, but I haven't gotten them yet. Now that I know we had more in common than I thought possible, I want to know more about my father, too."

"What do you know about him?"

"That he's dead. Mom would always change the subject when I brought him up" Dahlia answered with a sigh.

Carter nodded. She studied his body language and he looked uncomfortable.

"Did you know him?"

Carter didn't reply.

"Please, Carter. Can you tell me anything? A name?" Dahlia pleaded as she approached him. Her tone was of desperation and Carter found it difficult to say no.

"I knew him. His name was Lucas." Cater exhaled loudly.

"Thanks. At least that's something." She sighed. "I don't think I'm going to find anything up here, Carter."

"I'm following your lead" he replied.

Dahlia pivoted sideways and took a step. She felt herself lose balance and squealed; in a blink, she was face to face with Carter and Dahlia burst into laughter.

"You alright?" he chuckled as Dahlia gained her composure.

"Yeah" she replied. "That's what I get for not paying attention. Thanks."

"No problem."

Dahlia found herself staring at him like she stared at Ronan - except Carter returned that stare. Part of her wanted to pull away - the part that told her that she had feelings for Ronan. The other part told her that she could like two guys at the same time, and she didn't have a concrete relationship yet.

Carter pulled Dahlia to him, and his lips grazed hers. She pressed against him and melted into his embrace as their kiss grew deeper.

Dahlia pulled away quickly when Carter's phone rang.

"I'm sorry," he said as he pulled his cell phone out.

As Carter chatted on his phone, Dahlia looked at what caused her to trip. She only made out the first two letters on the cardboard box: *DI*. She inhaled and held her breath. She turned back to Carter who was still on the phone. Dahlia waited as he finished up his conversation.

When Carter hung up, Dahlia asked, "Is everything okay?"

"It was an invite to the movies. They all want you to come along" Carter replied.

"I'd rather stay here today."

"If you want company, I have no problem staying" he offered.

Dahlia smiled. "I appreciate that but go and have fun."

"You sure?"

"Yeah. I promise, the next time you go somewhere, I'll be there" Dahlia told Carter.

He grinned. "I'll hold you to that."

Dahlia laughed. "I know you will. I'll walk you out."

Carter led the way down the narrow staircase and Dahlia continued to follow him to the first floor and out to his car.

Before he got into his vehicle, Carter looked at Dahlia.

"If that was weird, I'm sorry. You finding out that I knew your parents, and then kissing you must seem...well, sort of creepy."

Dahlia laughed. "Actually, I'm not creeped out. If I was, I wouldn't have kissed you back."

"Good point."

"Plus, I feel comfortable with you."

"Same here" he replied.

"It'd be nice to have someone other than Gram to talk to" she hinted.

"Are you referring to your abilities?"

"Yes, I am."

"I may not talk much, but if you ever want to, let me know."

"I will," Dahlia said with a smile.

Carter got in his car and Dahlia watched him leave. She knew she was in trouble. She liked both Ronan and Carter, and the way she was starting to feel about Carter was just about equal to the way she felt about Ronan. To top it off, Dahlia felt guilty about kissing Carter now that he wasn't there.

Dahlia re-entered the house and immediately went back upstairs. She was tempted to look in that box and her pace picked up until she was standing in front of it. Dahlia picked it up and brought it directly under the light.

Good. You found it.

Dahlia looked at Juniper who was trotting up to her.

"You knew about this?" Dahlia asked him.

Why do you think I showed you where the door to the attic was?

It's so hard to hate him, Dahlia thought to herself.

"Thank you," she said, and she opened the box. Dahlia removed the garment on top which was a pale blue and gold knitted blanket that was beautifully made.

"Is this he only box, Juniper?" Dahlia asked the cat as she pulled out more items.

Yes.

Dahlia looked through Diana's awards from school, her high school diploma, old birthday cards, a large diary, and she eyed the photographs. She started going through them, and a smile formed as she watched her mother's teen years flash before her eyes.

Halfway through, she dropped the pile on the floor.

What did you find? Juniper meowed as he studied Dahlia's face.

Dahlia didn't answer him. She just stared at the picture in her hand.

18. UNVEILED

Dahlia was standing in the kitchen when Eve arrived home.

"Hi, honey. How was your day?" Eve asked her as she placed bags of groceries on the counter. Dahlia didn't reply.

"What's wrong, Dahlia?" she added.

"I found this today," Dahlia said. She slid the picture to her grandmother. Eve looked at it, and then looked back at Dahlia.

"I see you've been in the attic."

"I was, yes. I also found a diary that I've skimmed through. She was young when she wrote it and my father's name came up a lot, but he would because he was her best friend. What I'm upset about is that you know Ronan - you all do - and you didn't tell me! And he knows my mother! I'll deal with him on my own, but why didn't you tell me?!"

"It's not my place to tell you about Ronan. He has to tell you on his own."

"But he's human! How's this possible?!" Dahlia exclaimed.

Eve smiled softly. "Is he?"

"He has no energy, Gram, so-" Dahlia stopped herself. "He's carrying iron, isn't he?"

"He doesn't need to, dear. Ronan doesn't have energy" Eve replied.

"Why? I don't understand," Dahlia said impatiently.

"Dahlia, Ronan's unique. He's a vampire."

"A vampire?" she questioned Eve.

"Yes. I've known him for over three hundred years. Ronan and Diana were good friends."

"Why didn't he tell me?!" Dahlia exploded. "If he knew my mom, it should've been easy!"

"In his defense, have you told him about *your* abilities?"

"Well, no, but-"

"Why would it be any different for him? Ronan's been walking this planet for rive centuries. What makes you any different, Dahlia?"

Dahlia knew that Eve had a valid point.

"Is that why you pretended you didn't know him when he came to the house?"

"Would you want me to tell people that you drink blood to survive? That you've been alive for hundreds of years? That you have to watch people you know and are close to die over and over?"

"No" Dahlia groaned. "But I deserve to know the truth and *that's* why I'm upset with him. I-"

Eve pushed her car keys to Dahlia across the counter.

"He lives at the end of Madison Drive. You can't miss the house. Go talk to him. I know your angry right now, but let him explain," Eve interrupted her.

Dahlia grabbed the keys and hurried out of the house.

Dahlia parked on the roundabout beside Ronan's driveway. She stepped out of the car and walked up to his front door. She knocked and waited.

The door opened and Ronan looked surprised to see her.

"What are you doing here, Dahlia?" Ronan asked her.

"Why? Why didn't you tell me?" she blurted out.

"Tell you what?" he questioned.

"That you're a fucking vampire, Ronan!" Dahlia yelled. Ronan quickly pulled her inside and slammed the door.

"How the hell-"

"My grandmother told me after I found an old picture of my mom with you!"

"Great" he mumbled.

"Why wouldn't you tell me? You knew my mom, Ronan! You knew I'd understand!"

"It's not something you tell just anyone, Dahlia!"

"I'm not just anyone! You knew I'm Diana's daughter!"

"I was going to tell you, okay, but your friends don't leave you alone."

"Then pull me away! Why are guys so difficult? You guys don't take the easy route. There's always something! Did you think I wouldn't understand that you're not human? I'm not human, either."

"That's not it, Dahlia. I wasn't ready to tell you, yet."

"That's all you had to say," Dahlia said and sighed.

"Your friends don't make it easier."

"What's your deal them anyway?"

"I've known them since sixteen ninety-eight. I met them during the Salem Witch Trials, and we were all friends for many years, except for Carter. He never liked me. I was never welcome when it came to him, and I never will be.

"I was the closest to Eve, I was there when Diana was born and as she grew up we became great friends. Carter didn't like that, either."

"Where were you when my mom was locked in a room in someone's house when she was a kid?" Dahlia asked, crossing her arms. She was taking a leap with what she saw in her dream. It seemed so real.

Ronan went deadpan. "Who told you that?"

"You just did. So, where were you?" she asked again.

"I don't talk about that." His jaw locked and his body stiffened, He looked intimidating.

"Why?" She looked at him for a few seconds before continuing. "Look, I don't care what the others think about you. I only care about how I think of you, and I don't care if you're a vampire. I just wish you trusted me enough to tell me the truth."

"I never said I didn't trust you, Dahlia. I do trust you."

"It doesn't feel like it."

Ronan didn't reply and the awkward silence got uncomfortable.

"I should get home" she added.

"Yeah, that's a good idea" Ronan answered and opened the door for her.

Dahlia walked through the threshold and heard the door shut. She had more questions to ask him about her parents and about him being in Seattle, but Ronan never would've told her tonight. She noticed how his demeanor changed from his normal calm and suave to taut and unapproachable. She knew this - her dreams were real, and Ronan knew more than he wanted to share.

19. STRONG ADVICE

Dahlia turned onto her street; she was still upset and confused about what she discovered. She couldn't wrap her head around all of it, not yet at least.

As se rounded the corner, a large mass moved swiftly across the road. Dahlia swerved and slammed on the brakes.

"What the hell was that?" she exclaimed breathlessly. She got out of the car and looked into the darkness of the forest in front of her.

Dahlia's composure straightened when she saw it: a tall figure standing by a nearby tree. Its energy was unreadable.

"Ronan?" she asked.

No answer. Not even the slightest movement.

Dahlia took one step toward the front of the car.

Dahlia.

She stopped dead in her tracks and watched as the figure took a step closer. It was then that she knew it wasn't Ronan...or did she? He wasn't himself when she left his house.

Dahlia got back in the car and sped off toward home.

Dahlia entered the house and heard the television from the den. She left the keys on the counter and walked into the room off of the kitchen.

"How'd it go?" Eve asked her.

"He's frustrating! I told him I didn't care who he was or if he doesn't get along with my friends and I feel like he dismissed me! All I wanted was the truth and I told him that."

"You know the truth, Dahlia. What more do you want from him?"

I don't know the truth about everything, she thought to herself.

"Whose side are you on, Gram?"

Eve grinned. "I'm not on anyone's side, honey. I've known Ronan a long time and we've always seen eye to eye. Despite what Carter may think of Ronan, he's a good man. He was close to Diana, so don't forget that he's also dealing with her death. You need to give him a break and reconcile."

"Reconcile?"

"Yes, reconcile. Be the bigger person. Second chances are blessings, Dahlia."

Dahlia didn't reply to that statement. She said goodnight, grabbed the picture off the counter, and went upstairs. Juniper was sleeping on Dahlia's bed. His head popped up when she shut the door.

Are you done flipping out? Juniper yawned and stretched out his front legs.

"I wasn't flipping out" she replied as she removed her shoes.

Right, and I'm the King of France.

Dahlia rolled her eyes and placed the picture on her desk. She changed out of her jeans and pulled on a pair of flannel pajama bottoms before settling down with the diary. She was on a mission to find out about the dreams she kept having.

As soon as Dahlia came across Ronan's name, she grabbed her cell phone from the bedside table and found his number. He didn't answer her call, so she left him a voicemail. Then she left him a text message.

Dahlia checked her phone more than she read. Ronan wasn't answering her at all.

"How can I be the bigger person if he won't answer me?!" Dahlia exclaimed.

Stop bothering him.

"I'm not trying to bother him."

That doesn't mean you're not.

Dahlia narrowed her eyes at him.

Your dog would say the same thing.

"I doubt that."

You're arguing with a cat.

"There's nothing else to do" Dahlia mumbled. She looked at her phone one more time before putting it back on the table.

20. FALLOUT

Dahlia dreaded the want of going to school: Ronan. He didn't answer her texts or calls all weekend, and she was afraid of what he was going to say when she asked him why he never replied. She cared about him regardless of what was going on. Those were feelings she couldn't shut off.

She didn't talk much on the way to school with Nina. Dahlia knew she'd get bombarded later. She was more worried about her confrontation with Ronan.

Dahlia and Nina walked into school and went their separate ways. She had to tell Trent, Reid, and Carter that she was on good terms with them. Eve had called Carter about what Dahlia found out about Ronan. Dahlia didn't want to talk about Ronan with those who didn't have a care in the world for him.

Throughout the day, Dahlia looked for Ronan, but he didn't show up. Did she really get to him that bad? She wanted her words to sink in, but she didn't want him to disappear.

Dahlia was on her way to her locker when she overheard Kate make a comment about Ronan not returning to school because of her. Dahlia could feel her blood boil and if she wasn't holding her books, her hands would be in fists.

"She's bored. Don't listen to her," said a voice to her right. Dahlia turned her head and saw Carter.

"Does she realize that people are allowed to miss school? What's *wrong* with that girl?"

"That's just Kate. She makes a big deal out of nothing" Carter replied.

"It takes great restraint not to say something to her."

"It's not worth it."

Carter walked with Dahlia to her locker.

"You shouldn't let Pierce get to you, either," he added as Dahlia opened the locker door. She turned and looked at him.

"I know you don't like Ronan, but don't expect me to hate him, too. He's done nothing to me" Dahlia told her friend.

"I don't expect that at all."

"That's not the vibe I get from you, Carter." Dahlia turned back to her locker and put her things away. "I have to work on the murals for the dance. I'll see you later." Dahlia closed her locker door and walked away without a glance at Carter. A rush of realization consumed him: Dahlia cared about the vampire.

Carter found Dahlia in the large art room. A large mural covered the left wall that was unfinished of a large rickety Victorian house. Dahlia was taking paint off of a shelf and didn't seem phased by Carter in the room.

"Are you kidding me, Dahlia?"

She looked at him in bewilderment.

"Excuse me?" she asked him.

"You actually have feelings for that leech?!" Carter exclaimed in anger.

For a split second, Dahlia thought she saw Carter's eyes change color.

"He has a name!" she snapped at him.

"Why?! How?!" Carter exploded. "You don't even know him, Dahlia!"

"How do you know what I know about him? Have you been watching me, Carter?" Dahlia kept as calm as she could, but she wanted to unleash her anger on him. Carter's breathing was heavy, and he didn't answer.

"Have you?" she asked him again.

No reply.

Dahlia sighed. "Regardless if you are or not, my feelings for Ronan are no concern of yours. I don't care how close you were to my mother. My feelings belong to *me* and me only. I'm sorry if that pisses you off, but you can't control who you're attracted to. I don't need your input."

Carter exhaled loudly. "I guess not. Don't come crying to me when you get hurt. And you will."

He stormed out of the room.

21. A STANDSTILL

Dahlia entered the house and placed her bag by the stairs. She checked her cell phone for any messages, but there was nothing. She sighed and walked into the kitchen. Juniper was lying on the counter, purring like crazy.

"Faker," said Dahlia as she opened the refrigerator. Juniper snarled and turned his body to face the other way. Dahlia snickered and grabbed the pitcher of iced tea. She heard her cell phone go off and she nearly dropped the pitcher on the tile. She took out her phone with her free hand quickly in hopes it was Roman. She sighed when it was no such luck.

"Hey, Nina" Dahlia answered. She grabbed a glass out of the cupboard and poured herself some iced tea.

"*(Hey! You didn't talk much today. Are you alright?)*...I'm fine...*(Dahl, I can tell you're lying even over the phone)*..."

Dahlia rolled her eyes and put the pitcher back in the refrigerator.

"It's nothing I can't deal with, I promise...*(Do you want to talk about it?)*...Not really, no."

She could picture the look on Nina's face and felt guilty about her response.

"*(Well, if you do want to talk, let me know)*...I will...*(I'm going shopping with Lily for the dance tomorrow after school. You want to come?)*...Sure! That sounds like fun!"

Dahlia smiled. She needed a distraction, and shopping for a costume would be the perfect one.

"*(Perfect! Right after school, okay?)*...Oh, I can't right after. I still have to make the finishing touches on the murals for the Gym...*(That's no problem, Dahl. We can go once you're done. We'll have dinner, too)*...Sounds perfect. I'll see you in the morning, okay? I have homework to do and dinner to start…*(See you in the morning! Have a good night)*…You, too, Nina."

Dahlia hung up and grabbed her backpack by the stairs. She then set up a space at the kitchen table to do her homework and looked around to figure out what to make for dinner.

At half past six, Eve arrived home. The smells of rosemary, basil, and chicken permeated the first floor of the house and Eve made her way into the kitchen. She saw her granddaughter at the center island carefully cutting fresh mozzarella.

"What are you making? It smells wonderful" Eve asked.

"Mom used to make it for me. It's a chicken caprese salad with basil, olive oil, tomatoes, fresh mozzarella, spinach, mixed greens, and chicken that I quickly marinated in rosemary and Italian dressing." Dahlia looked at Eve and smiled. She had Diana's smile.

"Your mother was always in this kitchen experimenting with fruits and vegetables from the garden."

"We had a little garden in Seattle. It was her pride and joy. I was forced to help her weed and plant when I was younger." Dahlia laughed. "I'd pretend I was asleep, so I didn't have to go outside, or I'd go to a friend's house. She caught on. But eventually, I got into it a couple of years ago."

"Just like your mother. She didn't want to help me at first, but it grew on her. I think it fascinated her to be honest with you. You're more like her than I thought."

"I don't think I am, though" Dahlia replied.

"You absolutely are! You have her smile, you have her strong will, you have her strength-"

"I have her power" Dahlia interrupted.

"You have her ability, but that doesn't mean your power's the same. Her father was human, so her power wouldn't have had the potential like yours."

Dahlia stood up straighter. "My father was a witch?"

Eve simply nodded.

"I want to know more about him, Gram, but no one will tell me! Please tell me something! Anything!"

"Your father is a conversation you don't want to hear, honey."

"Yes, I do."

"You also have Diana's stubbornness. Talking about him won't help. He's better left forgotten."

"I've never met him, so how can I forget?"

"Once you hear something or see something, Dahlia, it can't be unheard or unseen no matter how hard you try."

"So, he's going to remain a mystery?"

"For now, yes" Eve replied.

"Will you *ever* tell me?"

"When you're ready. That's a discussion for another day."

"I'll hold you to that, Gram."

"I won't forget. My memory's sharp. I'm also ready to eat whenever the food's ready."

"Take a seat and I'll bring everything to the table."

Eve grabbed the iced tea from the refrigerator and put it on the table. She grabbed two glasses and placed them in front of the chairs they would sit in.

Dahlia served the food family style and sat down to enjoy it.

"How's school?" Eve asked as she served herself some chicken.

"It's good. I'm almost done with the murals for the dance, and they look fantastic. Oh, I don't know when I'll be home tomorrow because I'm going shopping with Nina and Lily for our dresses."

"Do you know what you want to be yet?"

"It's a masquerade. Everyone wears a mask. Nice dresses and Venetian masks."

"Masquerade. That sounds like it's going to be lovely. I've been to a few myself in my hay day. Do you have a date?" Eve cut up her chicken and salad.

"No date" Dahlia replied quietly. Her eyes drifted to her plate, and she began to push the food around.

"But you want one, correct?"

"I don't need one."

Eve smiled. "That's not what I asked."

Dahlia sighed and looked at her grandmother. "I'd like one, but Ronan's avoiding me, and Carter's pissed at me because I like Ronan!"

"Carter and Ronan. They've had their differences and they always will."

"I like them both, Gram."

"That's apparent, and in a perfect world you could have both, but the world we live in isn't perfect. You'll have to pick one, dear," Eve said matter-of-factly.

"I know." Dahlia sighed loudly. "I care about both of them, but...it's different with Ronan. I can't explain it. They're on different levels."

"It sounds like you know who you want already, sweetheart."

"I don't want to hurt anyone. It would be so much easier if I didn't feel the way I did for Ronan, but I can't turn it off. Now he won't even talk to me! I'll fix what happened between Carter and I tomorrow, but Ronan's going to be a challenge."

"When it comes to making choices like this, someone always gets hurt, even when you try to make it painless. Call him again."

"I have been! He won't answer! I've been leaving messages, but he's being a pain in the ass!"

"Keep calling him, Dahlia."

"But-"

"Just keep calling him. He can't hide forever. Not in this town."

Once the dinner dishes were picked up, washed, dried, and put away, Dahlia went upstairs with her backpack. She changed into something more comfortable to wear to bed before dialing Ronan's number. She sighed when it went to voicemail.

"Ronan, it's me again. Stop being difficult and talk to me please. You know my number. Use it."

Dahlia plugged her phone into the charger and stared at it. She didn't notice Juniper enter the room.

You think watching it will do anything?

"Shut up, feline."

Juniper jumped up on the bed and rested in front of Dahlia's stomach.

You're staring at it like it's going to do a trick.

"I just want it to ring, that's all."

And looking at it will make it ring?

Dahlia looked at Juniper annoyed. "Are you done?"

I'm never done. He turned on his side. *Scratch my stomach.*

"You're a rude little thing, why should I?"

You have nails and being rude is my nature. Cats are independent, dogs are stupid.

"Dogs are loyal, Juniper," Dahlia said on the defense.

So are cats.

"Not like dogs are, sorry."

Juniper growled but remained on his side. Dahlia hoped that the comment would cause Juniper to leave the room, but she was wrong. She scratched his stomach as she continued to stare at her cell phone.

***

Dahlia woke up to her alarm clock buzzing in her ear. She turned it off and looked at her phone. No messages or missed calls. She took a deep breath and got out of bed.

She took her shower and got ready for the day. Dahlia thought about texting Ronan, but she was sick of being rejected by him.

Once at school, Ronan was a no show and Carter kept his distance from Dahlia. She shrugged it off and tried to focus on something else. That was more difficult than she thought.

After her last class, Dahlia found Carter at his locker. She approached him and said hello.

"What can I do for you, Dahlia?" Carter asked. It wasn't the usual tone he used when he spoke to her.

"I wanted to apologize about yesterday. I didn't mean to lose my temper with you, and I know that you and Ronan don't get along, but you crossed a line. I lost my cool and I'm sorry" Dahlia apologized.

Carter looked surprised. He thought he'd be the one to say sorry first.

"I didn't expect that" he replied.

"I'm sick of being avoided by Ronan and I don't need to add you to the list," said Dahlia.

"It wouldn't have lasted" Carter admitted. There was a hint of a smile on his face.

"So, we're okay?"

"We're okay" he answered.

Dahlia smiled. "On that note, will you go to the dance with me?"

Carter's eyebrows raised. "Really?"

Dahlia nodded.

"How can I say no?"

"Great! I have to get going, but I'll see you later."

"Sounds good."

Dahlia kissed him on the cheek and started toward the art room.

"Suck on that, blood sucker" Carter mumbled with a grin.

As Dahlia did the finishing touches on the murals, her mind reeled with thoughts of Ronan and Carter. She cared about them both, and just when she thought she liked them both on the same level, Ronan beat Carter by a hair. She was beside herself. While one cooperated with her, the other one wouldn't.

Dahlia walked outside to see Lily, Nina, and Reid waiting for her.

"Hey, Dahl!" Nina greeted her. They all smiled at her.

"I'm sorry it took so long, guys. I'm ready when you are. You coming along, Reid?" Dahlia asked him.

"Oh, no. This is a girl's night out. The guys wear suits and I have plenty."

"Let's get the ball rolling, ladies," said Lily and she walked toward the parking lot.

"That's my cue to leave." Reid kissed Nina. "Have fun." He waved and started walking in the opposite direction of the parking lot.

"Ready?" Nina asked her friend with a smile.

Dahlia nodded and walked toward Nina's car.

"I want that," Dahlia said suddenly.

"You want what?" asked Nina.

"What you and Reid have. I want that."

"You will!" she exclaimed and put her arm around Dahlia's shoulders.

"Eventually. Does the curse faze you?"

"I don't look at it like a curse, Dahl. I get to spend the rest of my life with Reid. Our love's the same. We may change our appearance, but the way we feel about each other never changes."

"Your names change, too." Dahlia grinned. Nina chuckled.

"We always find each other regardless."

"That's beautiful."

Lily, Dahlia, and Nina pile into Nina's vehicle and she sped off.

22. TORN

Dahlia walked into the house with her dress wrapped up and a bag in her hand. She could hear the television on in the den and hung her dress over the banister.

"I'm home" Dahlia announced as she made her way to the kitchen.

"Did you have fun?" she heard her grandmother ask.

Dahlia grabbed a bottle of water out of the refrigerator and joined Eve.

"I did. I found a dress to wear and a mask to match."

"What color?"

"Dark red. The mask is black with red, white, and black feathers. The heels are black."

"Lovely. I can't wait to see you all dressed up. What time will Carter be here to pick you up?"

Dahlia's eyebrows raised. "How do you know I'm going with Carter?"

Eve smiled. "Grandmothers know things."

"I guess *so*," Dahlia mumbled. "I'm excited, though. Ronan still won't answer my calls or texts and I know I'll have fun with Carter."

"Yes, you will."

"I'm going upstairs. I'll see you tomorrow, Gram."

"Goodnight, dear."

Dahlia walked upstairs to her room with her new dress and accessories. She was surprised that Juniper wasn't asleep on her bed, but it was only a matter of time before he graced her with his presence.

Dahlia checked her phone one more time, but she had an inkling that Ronan didn't leave anything for her; she was right. However, she *did* have a text message from her aunt. Dahlia smiled when she saw a picture of Clark and his goofy grin.

"Soon, boy," she said. She sent the picture to her e-mail to print out later and replied to the message. Involuntary tears fell from her eyes as she told her aunt to give Clark a hug and kiss for her.

***

Dahlia stood in front of her full-length mirror in her dress for the Masquerade. Her brown hair was curled at the ends and pulled halfway up with bobby pins. Her make-up was flawless, and she had her mask in her hand. She wore a white gold chain with a diamond pendant that her grandmother let her borrow to accentuate the elegance of her neck.

Dahlia heard the doorbell, and she made her way downstairs. Carter was talking to Eve at the door and Dahlia was instantly noticed. Both Eve and Carter smiled as she finished descending the stairs.

"Absolutely beautiful," Eve said.

"Thank you, Gram. The necklace is a great touch" Dahlia replied.

"I agree." Eve looked at Carter who was in a trance as he looked at Dahlia. "Don't you have something for her?"

Dahlia chuckled when Carter was caught off guard. He presented her with a corsage of red roses and baby's breath. The color of the flowers matched her dress perfectly.

"It's beautiful. Thank you." Dahlia smiled as Carter slipped the corsage onto her wrist.

"You two have fun" Eve told them after snapping a picture of them. She opened the door.

"We will." Carter turned to Dahlia. "After you." He smiled. Dahlia returned the smile, said goodbye to Eve, and stepped through the threshold.

Carter and Dahlia walked toward the gymnasium. Music blared throughout the hallway and there were teenagers everywhere.

"What's wrong?" Carter asked Dahlia suddenly. She looked at him in confusion and pulled her arm from his.

"What do you mean? Nothing's wrong."

Carter gave her a little smile. "Did you forget that I'm an Empath? Your emotions are overwhelming right now."

"How overwhelming?" Dahlia questioned him.

"I have no idea what song is playing. It's distressing."

Dahlia sighed. "Beyonce's Crazy in Love is playing. I'm sorry. It's not you who's making me feel like this, Carter" she admitted.

"I know who it is, Dahlia."

"And I don't want to talk about him. I'm here with you," Dahlia said firmly.

Carter nodded and Dahlia looped her arm around his once again. Although she made it clear to him that he wasn't the cause of her unhappiness, her emotions were difficult to ignore.

Carter and Dahlia walked into the gym. The murals looked fantastic and eerie with the lighting that was chosen to showcase them. Every guy wore a suit of some color with a simple eye mask, and the girls wore a variety of styled dresses with beautiful masks. It didn't look like a high school dance.

Dahlia spotted their friends and they joined them at the table they were all sitting at. Everybody complimented each other and while some decided to dance, the others stayed back and talked.

Dahlia's mood was starting to change. The more she conversed, the better she felt. She even joined Nina and Lily on the dance floor for a couple of songs as the guys watched.

Dahlia and Carter were in the middle of a slow dance when Carter suddenly stiffened.

"What's wrong?" Dahlia asked him. Carter told her to turn her head toward the gymnasium entrance. Dahlia did what he said, and she saw Ronan. He was dressed in black and white with a white eye mask. Dahlia's breath caught when Ronan started to walk toward her.

"Dance with him" Carter instructed Dahlia. She looked at him incredulously.

"What?" she asked exasperated.

"Obviously he's here to see *you*, Dahlia. It's a dance, so dance with him."

Dahlia furrowed her brows as Carter walked away from her.

"That was nice of him. Trouble in paradise?" a voice asked behind her. Dahlia took a deep breath and turned around.

"*Now* you're talking to me? That's sweet of you."

A new song began to play, and Ronan pulled her close. He wrapped his arms around her waist; Dahlia placed her arms around his neck, but she wasn't done talking.

"What's going on with you, Ronan? You've been ignoring me, even after I told you that I don't care what you are. It's not hard to pick up a phone or text me back."

"I know," Ronan said.

"That's it? That's all you have to say?"

"What else do you want me to say, Dahlia?"

"I want the truth! I want you to talk to me, Ronan!" Dahlia realized that she was getting loud when Carter, Reid, and Trent all stood up from the table. Lily and Nina stayed seated, but there were looks of worry on their faces.

"Look, getting too close to me isn't in your best interest."

"Oh, really? Why's that?" Dahlia asked, pulling away from him.

"I made a promise to your mother to protect you if anything happened to her. I can't protect you if we get too close" Ronan replied after he pulled her to him again.

Dahlia stared at Ronan like he had ten heads. Her face felt hot, and she wanted to hit him. It was even more difficult since she had feelings for him, but her anger was rapidly drowning out those feelings.

"I'm going to tell you what you're going to do. I want you to forget about me, Ronan. I don't need you or your damned protection! I want you to leave me alone! We'll both be happier" Dahlia spat at him and pushed him away.

Ronan was taken aback. "Dahlia-"

"Shut up."

Dahlia walked away, leaving him alone on the dance floor. Ronan watched as Dahlia's friends followed after her.

"Good job" Carter told Ronan on his way out.

THE EDGE OF DARKNESS — A.L. FLAGG

23. FRAY

Dahlia was leaning against Carter's car when Carter walked outside. The others were standing back at a distance watching her.

"Usually when one of your friends is upset, you console them," Carter said to the group.

"That's difficult when your friend wants to be alone" Lily replied.

"Why don't you guys go and enjoy the dance" Carter told everyone. He made his way over to his car and Dahlia looked at him.

"I know you want to be alone right now, but that's not going to happen when I'm around," Carter told Dahlia.

"I don't want to go back in there" she whispered.

"What do you want to do then?"

"Can you bring me home?"

"If that's where you want to go then yes."

Dahlia nodded and walked around to the passenger side door. Carter unlocked the car and they both got inside.

"Do you want to talk about it?"

"No," Dahlia said firmly. Carter nodded and started the vehicle.

The ride to Dahlia's was quiet. Carter felt how hurt and angry she was. He didn't like seeing Dahlia without a smile on her face, and right now he wanted nothing more than to rip out Ronan's heart and feed it to him for hurting her.

Carter walked Dahlia to the door, and she thanked him for doing so.

"I'm sorry about what happened at the dance, Dahlia. If I knew he was just going to upset you, I would've never let you-"

"It's okay, Carter. Water under the bridge. He finally told me the truth" Dahlia interrupted him.

"You didn't deserve that. The bastard could've waited to tell you in private at least."

"What's done is done, but I don't disagree with you."

"Are you going to be okay?"

"I'm stronger than I look" Dahlia replied.

Carter grinned. "I know."

"You're a great friend. Thank you." Dahlia hugged Carter. He felt her anger diminishing, but the hurt still remained.

"I wish there was something I could do to make you feel better," said Carter.

"You're doing just fine" Dahlia answered. She chuckled and Carter smiled. "I should go in." Dahlia pulled away. "Thank you for going to the dance with me. I'm sorry we left early. You should go back and enjoy it."

Carter grinned. "I don't need to go back. All I'd do is sit on the sidelines anyway. I had all the fun I needed. Plus, watching Reid and Nina gets old."

Dahlia laughed. "They're in love. I've never met anyone more in love than them two. I want that someday."

"You'll find it, trust me."

The way Carter looked at her made the butterflies in her stomach flutter. Carter felt how nervous Dahlia was and he pulled back from what he was planning to do. He knew the feelings were there, but he knew she struggled with her feelings for Ronan as well.

"If you want to talk, you know my number," Carter said suddenly.

"Thanks. I'll talk to you later." Dahlia kissed him on the cheek and went inside. She jumped when she saw Eve standing by the staircase.

"Hey."

"You're home early," said Eve with a worried look on her face.

"Yeah."

Eve nodded. Dahlia knew by her grandmother's expression that she already knew what happened.

"I don't want to talk about it" Dahlia added.

"We don't have to. Go unwind and I'll bring you some tea."

"Thanks." Dahlia forced a small smile and walked upstairs to her bedroom. She saw Juniper sprawled out on her bed and Dahlia immediately went to her pile of clean clothes for something to change into.

Someone called you.

"Thanks."

Dahlia walked into the bathroom and closed the door. She changed out of her dress, hung it up, and removed the make-up from her face.

When she stepped out of the bathroom, Dahlia saw the cup of tea on her night stand next to her cell phone. She sat down, took a sip of her hot beverage, and checked her phone. She was surprised to see that the call was from Ronan, and that he left a message. She tapped into her voicemail to see what he had to say, but all that was said was her name and he hung up. Ronan sounded distressed and that's how Dahlia wanted him to feel. She had no intention of calling him back. She had no intention of talking to anyone.

24. ORIGIN

Over the weekend, Dahlia had gotten a few calls from Carter and Nina. They wanted to make sure she was okay after what happened after what had transpired at the dance, and all Dahlia wanted was to be left alone. She confided in her aunt and grandmother, and even told Clark. Dahlia tried to keep busy to keep her mind off of Ronan.

On Monday morning, Dahlia wasn't asked about the dance by her friends. She saw Kate glance at her off and on all day and snicker, but Dahlia let it go. She didn't expect Ronan to show up and wasn't surprised when he didn't.

Dahlia didn't do much talking at all. There was nothing to say. Not even Carter said much, but Dahlia did exchange a few smiles here and there with him. She needed more than a couple days to sort everything out.

***

Dahlia stood in the cream-colored hallway again. The art that was once on the walls were replaced by pictures of Diana and of herself.

Smoke filled the house and Dahlia turned left. She could see bright orange flames roaring from the kitchen and the smoke was turning black.

Her mother's name was being called in an eerily calm manner. Dahlia couldn't tell where the person calling Diana was. She heard scuffling upstairs and Dahlia climbed the staircase.

Dahlia could hear a baby crying at the end of the hall. She hurried down the smoke-filled corridor, past the room her mother was held in and turned left into a large bedroom. It was a nursery. Her nursery.

Diana was holding the baby close to her as she tried to open the window with her free hand. She was trying to quiet the baby as Diana's name was being called over and over. There was nothing Dahlia could do to help her mother. She could see the tears run down Diana's face and she wanted to know who it was that was taunting her.

"Give me the baby, Diana," said a voice behind Dahlia. She turned around, but there was no one there.

"You'll never have her" Diana replied in a low tone.

There was an explosion of light in the doorway and Dahlia could only make out a silhouette.

"Give her to me."

"You'll have to take her from my cold dead fingers, Lucas."

Dahlia heard him laugh menacingly. Now she knew who was after them…her own father. She needed to know why.

A glow was coming from his hands and was growing larger as she watched. He managed to keep his face hidden well. Dahlia looked back at her mother and saw the look on her face – the look of a fighter. She wasn't going to give up her child willingly…or easily.

The bureau to Dahlia's right suddenly burst into flames less than a foot from Diana. The crib against the left side wall was engulfed *in fire seconds later. Diana cradled the baby to her chest as Lucas watched her with hungry eyes.*

"Diana." He enjoyed tantalizing her.

It was the shattering of glass from the window that made Dalia jump out of her skin. Lucas screamed out in anger; Diana disappeared through the window and Dahlia didn't see how she got out.

Dahlia ran downstairs through thick smoke and tall flame and out the front door. When she turned around, Dahlia saw that the house was deluged in bright orange. The smoke signals were as high as the trees as Dahlia stared at her first home burn.

Dahlia woke up to Juniper purring in her ear. She got up and stretched before going into the bathroom. She washed her face, brushed her teeth, and re-entered her room.

As Dahlia went through her drawers, she kept glancing at the old photograph attached to her vanity. She stopped shuffling through clothes and looked at the picture carefully. Her eyes widened when she was hit with the realization that the house she's been dreaming about is the same house in the photograph.

After she got dressed, Dahlia flew down the stairs to find her grandmother. She didn't find Eve in the den, so Dahlia walked out to the greenhouse. Eve was watering her tomato plants.

"Good morning, Dahlia." Eve looked at her granddaughter's face, and when she saw the look on Dahlia's face, her smile faltered. "What's wrong?"

"I've been having these dreams about a house. The one last night allowed me to see the outside of it and I've seen the house before…in the old picture I found in the attic. And the dreams are-"

"How long have you been having these dreams, Dahlia?" Eve interrupted her.

"Since I got here, why?"

"Tell me about them."

The look on Eve's face made Dahlia nervous.

"Are you okay?"

"Just tell me about your dreams, Dahlia." Eve said it with such urgency.

"Okay, well, the first one I was in the cream-colored hallway. They all start out like that actually, but it didn't look familiar. The décor was from the seventies in the first two dreams. I remember a giant staircase, a closet that hid a key to a room upstairs, and a monster of a woman sending me upstairs with a tray of food.

"The room upstairs only had a pigment of light. In the first dream, I didn't see the girl's face, but in the second one I saw that it was mom. That evil woman kept pulling me out of the room, though! But last night…last night's was-"

"What about it?" Eve interrupted.

"The house was on fire. Mom was upstairs in the nursery holding me, trying to get out. Her name was being called in this creepy, calm way. I never saw his face, but I saw his outline. He set the room on fire after mom told him he couldn't have me. His laugh was sinister. Then the window shattered, and mom was gone. I went outside and watched the house burn. Then I woke up."

"Why didn't you tell me about these dreams?"

"I didn't think they meant anything…until Ronan kind of told me."

"What did he tell you?" she asked immediately as she took a step forward.

"I brought up something about mom being locked up in a room and if Ronan was her best friend, why didn't he save her. He got upset. I knew then that those dreams were real. It was a shot in the dark at getting an answer and it worked."

Eve didn't say anything.

"You need to tell me everything. I'm lost in the dark here!"

"Come."

Dahlia followed Eve to the patio, and they sat down at the table.

"Those dreams are real. In fact, they're memories."

"Whose?" Dahlia asked.

"Your father's" Eve answered.

"How?"

"He has the ability to project his memories into others."

"So…I was seeing things through *his* perspective in the dreams?" Dahlia questioned incredulously.

"Yes, which means he's close."

"But wait…that doesn't make sense. In last night's dream, I saw his outline. I was myself in that dream. Explain that."

"His power is a lot stronger than we thought. Have you had any odd run-ins lately? Anything seem off to you?"

"Besides Ronan's behavior you mean?"

"Besides that."

Dahlia thought a minute. "The night I went to Ronan's. I was driving when something ran out across the road. I pulled over because I thought it might've been Ronan, but it wasn't. I saw a figure and heard my name. I was so creeped out, so I took off." Dahlia paused. "That was him, huh? My father?"

Eve nodded.

"What does he want?" Dahlia added.

"You, honey. That last memory you saw was an attempt to take you for himself and kill your mother in doing so."

"Why does he want me so bad? I doubt its love."

"Diana knew. Her intent was to get you out of Broken Bay as fast as possible, and she did. I didn't tell a soul where you went, but-"

"He found us" Dahlia interrupted. "And he killed my mother."

Eve looked at her granddaughter with saddened eyes.

"So, that house-"

"It belonged to Lucas's parents. He grew up there and after Lucas and Diana got married, she moved in. You didn't live there long."

"Why would mom live in a house where she was kept prisoner?!" Dahlia asked in disgust.

"She loved your father," Eve said simply.

"That blows me away! I can't believe that *his* parents allowed that marriage to happen!"

"Your grandparents left the island. The house was left to Lucas."

"That explains it then, huh?" Dahlia sighed and could feel a headache building. "How did mom get out of the house that night?"

"How do you think? Ronan."

"Ronan? Ronan saved us?" Dahlia questioned her.

"He did. If you want to know more, you have to talk to *him*."

"I don't want to talk to him right now." Another thought hit her. "If Lucas is in town, why hasn't he gotten to me yet?"

"He's a very intelligent being, Dahlia. He's always two steps ahead of the rest."

"It surprises me that he hasn't just grabbed me on the way into the house or something."

Eve smiled. "He can't come onto this property, dear. I have a very powerful charm on it, so you're safe here. He has a plan of his own, so stay on your guard" Eve warned her. This made Dahlia nervous.

"I want to see this house," Dahlia said. "I don't know why, but I think I need to see it. Is there anything left of it?"

"Yes. The foundation still stands. Charms can help with damage."

Dahlia suddenly grew angry. "Why wasn't a charm put on my house in Seattle then?!" she exploded.

"Honey, Diana didn't want one," Eve said calmly.

"What?"

"She was confident that she could protect you. She didn't want magic to be a part of your life, so she sheltered you from it. I offered my protection, but she turned me down."

"And now look. She's gone and my father's after me."

"Give Diana some credit, Dahlia. She kept you alive. She kept you safe. She did what she found was best for you and she did a great job if I do say so myself."

"What she should've done is sought out refuge here knowing that we would've been protected! She'd still be alive!"

Eve placed her hand on Dahlia's to stop it from shaking. "You're upset because you miss her, but that anger will subside. I miss her, too, honey. There's nothing we can do about the choices she made. So, if you want to go to the house, I'll take you."

Dahlia nodded.

The house was secluded in the woods down a long winding drive. It was falling apart, but the home didn't look horrible for being involved in a fire. Whatever charm was used, it was doing its job keeping it up. The paint was faint, and the shutters were on its hinges. The vines along the foundation were out of control. It was the house from Dahlia's dreams.

"I'm not going in there with you, but I'll wait out here," said Eve.

Dahlia got out of the car and stared at the house. She took a deep breath before proceeding toward the front door.

25. BREATHE AGAIN

Dahlia entered the broken-down home. She was standing in the same hallway that she stood in her dreams. The walls were no longer creamed colored, but her memory was sharp.

She found the large staircase and had the urge to see if the key was in the closet where she found it before. Out of curiosity, Dahlia had to look. The key was gone, and she wasn't surprised.

Dahlia looked up the staircase to the second floor. She climbed the stairs slowly; the walls were blackened, and she was cautious of where she was stepping. At the top of the landing, she could barely breathe.

She found herself entering the room her mother was kept prisoner. The room was smaller than she remembered, but it was as she remembered. She walked over to the vanity and ran her fingers along the charred furniture. She looked at the dust covered mirror and ran her pointer finger across it. She turned around slowly and walked out of the room.

Dahlia entered her old bedroom. She saw what was left of the burnt bureau and crib and the broken window. Dahlia heard a car start and she looked out through the window. Eve's vehicle was gone.

"That's just perfect. Thanks, Gram" Dahlia mumbled.

"I told her she could leave," said a voice behind Dahlia. She jumped slightly and whipped around. Ronan was leaning against the threshold.

Dahlia crossed her arms. "What are you doing here?" she asked him.

"Eve called me. She told me you were here" he answered as he stepped into the room.

"Great. Did she tell you about my dreams, too?"

"She did."

Dahlia rolled her eyes. "Of course she did."

"You want answers, right?"

"That's all I've wanted! It's like pulling teeth to get people to tell me something!" Dahlia expressed.

"To start off, Lucas hates me."

"You seem to be quite popular around here" she answered.

"I'm willing to tell you everything because you deserve to know what you're dealing with, so I don't need the wise ass remarks, Dahlia."

"Then talk, Ronan. Spill."

Ronan took a deep breath. "Right after the wedding, your parents and I had an altercation with a few vampires. They were stronger than I anticipated, and Diana hit a few with witch flame, but Lucas ended up getting hit as well. Because the burn was so bad, the only way he could be saved was by me turning him."

Dahlia's eyes grew wide. "You turned my father into a vampire?"

"I had no choice! Diana begged me to help him, so I did! Except Lucas's power accelerated beyond anyone's expectations. He became power hungry, and his blood thirst was out of control. I helped him as much as I could, and so did Eve and the others, but he liked who he had become.

"Then Diana told everyone she was pregnant. We were worried that you were a vampire, but she became pregnant *before* I turned him.

"After the news of the pregnancy, Lucas did a complete one-eighty. He was the old Lucas again. We never saw him so happy. Diana was so excited to have the old Lucas back.

"When you were born, a friend of Eve's told us that your energy was incredibly strong. That was Lucas's eureka moment."

"What do you mean by his eureka moment?" Dahlia questioned him.

Ronan hesitated and looked away from her.

"What do you mean?" she asked again.

"You have no idea how hard this is" he whispered.

"Please. I need to know" she pleaded. Ronan looked at Dahlia and saw the desperation in her eyes.

"His priority wasn't to be a father. He wanted your power; he wanted that energy and Diana figured it out. She wanted you away from Lucas and asked me to help her."

It dawned on Dahlia suddenly. "Jesus, he's going to kill me, isn't he?"

Ronan's posture straightened and his expression went deadpan.

"I won't allow that to happen."

"That's his intent, right? And if he succeeded in killing my mother when I was a baby, he was going to raise me for a little bit and then kill me because he's a power-hungry asshole hybrid, correct?"

Ronan didn't answer her, but Dahlia knew that she was right.

"Why not just kill me now then? Why make me wait? I'm ready to meet this bastard because I have a few words for him!" Dahlia shouted. Ronan reached out to her, but she pushed him away.

"Dahlia."

"Just…I don't want to be touched right now. Tell me why he's waiting so long to get me." Dahlia ran her hands through her hair in frustration.

"A witch's power is fully matured at eighteen."

Dahlia chuckled. "Perfect. That gives me a week to live. Lucky number seven."

"I have something for you." Ronan went into his jacket and pulled out an envelope. He handed it to Dahlia, and she saw her mother's handwriting on it. He also pulled out something else: a long chain with a large black stone. The stone was encased by white gold in an intricate design.

"Is that mom's amulet?" Dahlia whispered.

"Yes. She gave this and the envelope to me to give to you. That's why I was in Seattle."

Dahlia put the amulet around her neck and removed the letter from the envelope.

"Dahlia-"

"You don't have to read it out loud" Ronan interrupted her.

"I want to. It says:

Dahlia,

I can't tell you how sorry I am that it's led to this. I tried to protect you to the best of my ability, but in the end, Lucas still found you.

You're so much stronger than you think you are. I wanted so badly to shield you from magic, but it's alive in you. As you grew up, I watched as you discovered your abilities when you didn't think I was looking. I saw everything. You truly are remarkable, and your power will only continue to grow stronger as you get older.

You need to trust those around you. Your grandmother will help you to reach your full potential. She's a wonderful teacher. Your friends (our friends) will be by your side, so don't push them away. If you need them, they'll be there. They were there for me through thick and thin. I asked Ronan to protect you because he protected me. I know what he's capable of and no one can guard you like he can. I trust him with every part of me and I hope you can, too. You need to trust yourself, my love. Never second guess yourself. You know what's best for you.

At one time, I loved your father. He was my best friend, but the change in him lost my love. He wasn't the man I fell for, but he did give me you and you'll never be a regret. You were my miracle. You have to stay strong and keep your head up. I'm always with you even if you can't see me. I'll always be here to watch over you, and one day you'll be with me again. I love you, Dahlia. You're the light in the darkness, so shine bright.

Love, Mom

Tears were running down Dahlia's face as she folded the letter.

"She knew he was going to kill her" she whispered.

"I tried to save her, but I was too late," said Ronan.

Dahlia looked at him. "You saved me, didn't you?"

Ronan nodded.

"That was twice."

"I keep my promises."

"Ronan, I do trust you. I understand why you pushed me away. I understand why you don't want to get too close to me, and if that's how it has to be between us, then that's how it is."

He chuckled and ran his right hand through his hair roughly.

"What?" Dahlia asked.

"I was wrong" he replied.

"About what?"

"Everything. For thinking no contact would be better and easier. Clearly it isn't! For avoiding your phone calls, your texts, making you cry, making you hate me, all of it!"

"I don't hate you."

"Oh, stop! Even I hate me!"

Dahlia grabbed Ronan's hands, forcing him to look at her.

"I was hurt and angry, but I didn't hate you. I could *never* hate you. I'm alive because of you, Ronan. I owe you my life."

"You don't owe me anything."

"Even if I don't, I'm who I am because you got me out of that house, and I'll always be grateful."

Ronan dropped Dahlia's hands and his own cupped her cheeks.

"I didn't expect this. I didn't expect…to care for you like I do. I thought that it would be the same type of friendship I had with Diana, but clearly it's not. I want more…I need more. I need *you*. I can't be away from you anymore, Dahlia. It's not in me."

Dahlia smiled. "We have that in common, Ronan. I need you, too, more than ever."

"And I'll always be here." Ronan leaned in and brushed his lips against Dahlia's.

26. STAY

Ronan pulled into Dahlia's driveway and put the vehicle in park.

"Didn't you say you had an aunt?" Dahlia asked, turning sideways in her seat.

"I did, but Rosalie is technically my caretaker. She's been with me for the last twenty years and takes care of the house. Occasionally, she's had to put me in check." Ronan smirked.

"So, she's *like* family to you."

"No, she *is* family" he replied.

"How did you two meet?"

"Well, *her* mother was good friends with Eve, and Rosie and I were introduced through them. I watched her grow up, get married, go through a divorce, and I brought her in to stay with me. She's very loyal."

"She knows the truth about you?"

"I don't hide anything from her," said Ronan.

"That's good. I'd like to meet her sometime."

Ronan caressed Dahlia's hand. "She'd love to meet you."

Dahlia smiled, but her smile started to diminish.

"What's wrong?" Ronan asked her.

"I turn eighteen in a week. I don't know what I'm going to do about my father yet. It's inevitable that I'm going to meet him. I want answers, but I…" she trailed off.

"I won't let him hurt you, Dahlia. You have my word."

Ronan pulled Dahlia into a close embrace. She felt his hands caress her back and his touch made her close her eyes. She could fall asleep in his arms.

He kissed her forehead as he pulled away.

"You're kicking me out, aren't you?" Dahlia asked with a playful smile. He returned the smile.

"Do you honestly think I'd kick you out?"

"Probably not" she chuckled.

"Of course not. I told Rosie I'd have dinner with her."

"That sounds nice. Enjoy yourself." Dahlia gave Ronan a peck on the lips and opened the door.

"I'll see you later."

"I know" she answered with a grin and got out of the car. She waved Ronan off and went in the house to be greeted by Eve.

"Hello there."

"It's nice to see that you two are getting along again," Eve said.

"Is that why you called him? So we'd work everything out?"

"I called him so you could get the answers you were looking for. And I see you found your mother's amulet in the midst as well."

Dahlia touched the amulet. "Mom gave it to Ronan to give to me."

"I'm glad she did. It's with its rightful owner now and soon you'll notice your strength in your power, especially your resurrection ability."

"Does the amulet already know who I am?"

"It knew you from the moment you put it on, honey." Eve smiled.

"I don't have to say a spell or anything?" Dahlia questioned.

"You watch a lot of movies" Eve chuckled. "I'll be making dinner soon. What do you feel like having?"

"I'm satisfied with a sandwich".

"How about some soup to go with that?"

"Perfect. I'll be down in a minute."

Dahlia climbed the stairs and went into her room to change her clothes. She looked around; Dahlia was unsure of how she was going to survive Lucas. She knew what his intentions were, but Dahlia wasn't sure if she was going to be strong enough to fight him. She wanted to be, but she didn't want to lie to herself. One thing she knew for sure - Dahlia wouldn't make it easy for Lucas to win.

***

Over the next few days, Carter and the others kept a close eye on Dahlia. Ronan didn't return to school, but Dahlia knew he was also watching. She was starting to become frustrated as they followed her everywhere, but she didn't have the heart to tell them to stop. She needed protection, but Dahlia needed to breathe, too.

It was October thirteenth, and everyone was on edge. Everyone except Dahlia. She was surprisingly calm and couldn't explain it, but it felt like there were even more eyes on her than the fourteen she knew about. She wanted to be alone, but there was no chance in that. As of midnight, she would be eighteen and Lucas would make his move.

After dinner, Dahlia retired to her room with Juniper. She changed into something more comfortable and took out her sketchbook. She made some finishing touches on Ronan's picture before starting something new.

"I'm going to draw you, Juniper."

Why?

"Why not?"

Juniper sniffed. *Make it good.*

"It'll be great, I promise" Dahlia assured the cat.

An hour into sketching, Dahlia heard a ping on her window.

Your boyfriend's here. Juniper yawned.

"My boyfriend?"

Dahlia got up and looked out onto the lawn. She spotted Ronan standing beneath her window. He waved and she lifted the framework.

"The front door works, too, you know" Dahlia chuckled.

"So will this if you let me in."

Dahlia stepped aside, and before she could blink, Ronan was closing the window.

"Well hello," she said. He looked at her and smiled.

"Hello."

"How long were you out there?"

"I'm out there every night" Ronan answered nonchalantly.

"You are?" Dahlia asked, furrowing her brow.

"I watch the house all night. Eve didn't tell you?" Ronan sounded surprised.

"She left out that little detail."

"Now you know." He laughed. He looked at Dahlia's sketchbook.

"Impressive," he added.

"Thank you. I hope Juniper approves. He's hard to please."

Juniper grunted and jumped off the bed. *All I want is sleep.* He squeezed through the crack in the door and Dahlia laughed.

"All that cat does is complain."

"Do you mind if I look at your other drawings?"

"Feel free. There's not many in there because the book is fairly new."

"This guy looks familiar." Ronan showed Dahlia the picture of him.

"I started it the day I met you. Then I lost the original in the fire, so I drew another one. It was a memento. Who knew I'd see you again?"

"It's amazing, except it's a misrepresentation of me."

"I don't agree" she argued.

Ronan looked at her. "Oh? You don't think the angel wings are a bit much?"

"No. This is how I see you."

"You see me as an angel?" he questioned her.

"Yeah, *mine*" Dahlia answered. She took the book from him and closed it. She got up and put it on the table; she looked back at Ronan who was staring at her.

"What?" she asked him.

"No one's ever told me that before."

Dahlia smiled. "There's a first time for everything, Ronan."

He stood up and stopped in front of her. "I'm not really good at this" Ronan whispered.

"Not good at what?" she whispered back.

"Being a boyfriend" he answered.

Dahlia grinned. "Is that what you are?"

"If you'll have me, yes." His forehead touched hers.

Dahlia tilted her head up and touched her lips to his. He pulled her closer and Dahlia's arms wrapped around his neck as their kiss grew deeper.

Ronan pulled her back toward the bed, and they fell upon the comforter. He pulled his head back and looked at Dahlia. His right hand slid the hair from her eyes.

"I think you'll be fine at being a boyfriend" she whispered.

Ronan chuckled and kissed Dahlia again.

"Can you stay the night?" Dahlia added.

"Like I do every other night?" Ronan grinned.

"Yes, but I'm asking you to stay *in* the house instead of staying *outside* the house." Dahlia returned the grin.

"I'll stay as long as you want me to" he told her as he ran his fingers through her hair.

"All night."

"No problem." He caressed her cheek before kissing Dahlia a third time.

Dahlia woke up to Juniper in her ear. She sat up to find Ronan gone but spotted a piece of paper on her bedside table.

"When did he leave?" Dahlia asked the cat.

A little while ago.

Dahlia reached over and grabbed the note.

HAPPY 18TH BIRTHDAY. I'LL SEE YOU LATER ON TONIGHT, ANGEL.

- -RONAN

Dahlia smiled. Dahlia's nerves were jumpy. She was eighteen and she was worried that she wouldn't be able to enjoy it.

27. ALL IS CRUMBLING

After getting dressed, Dahlia walked downstairs. The smell of bacon permeated the first floor. She walked into the kitchen to see Eve slaving away over the stove.

"Good morning, Gram."

Eve looked at Dahlia and smiled. "Happy birthday, sweetheart."

"Thank you. It smells good in here."

"Sit down. I made you breakfast, and I have something for you."

"You didn't have to do that" Dahlia told her grandmother.

"Nonsense! This is my first birthday with you! Now sit" Eve replied.

"This could be the last" Dahlia mumbled as she sat down at the head of the table.

"I don't want you talking like that, Dahlia."

"I know my father's intentions, and if he gets what he wants tonight, I'm dead. Don't tell me I'm wrong, either."

Eve brought Dahlia a large plate of food and placed it in front of her.

"He's not going to get what he wants, do you understand me? Lucas Rath won't get my granddaughter, too. I *refuse* to let that happen!"

"I plan to fight if need be. I know I have you, Ronan, and the others by my side."

"You're right, you do have all of us. That amulet will also help you. As evil as your father is, you have both of your parents' abilities and strength."

"I'm going to focus on my birthday and not on the fact that my father wants to kill me for my power."

Eve grinned. "Good idea." She pushed a package toward Dahlia. "I hope you like it."

Dahlia picked it up and tore the wrapping paper off of it. It was deep purple in color, hardcover, and thick.

"Is it a journal?" she asked. She fanned through the pages that were blank and lineless.

"In a sense, yes. It's a Book of Shadows. You put spells and anything relating to the magical world in it. Every witch should possess one."

Dahlia smiled and said "Thanks, Gram. It's great and I'll definitely utilize it." Dahlia started to cut up the breakfast sausage and pancakes on her plate.

"It'll come in handy I assure you. What are your plans for today?"

Dahlia took a bite of her scrambled eggs. "I don't know yet. I have a feeling I'll get a call from Nina. They don't seem like they would forget anything." She chuckled.

"You're right about that. Eat your breakfast and relax today. You only turn eighteen once."

After a long hot shower, Dahlia finished her drawing of Juniper. He didn't show his excitement, but Eve loved it. She found a frame for the picture and hung it up in the den.

Dahlia was bombarded with phone calls and text messages from friends back in Seattle, including Ryan. She was able to talk to Clark and her Aunt Kris as well.

Dahlia was woken up by her cell phone. Juniper grunted and shifted as Dahlia searched for the electronic device.

"Hello?" she asked groggily.

"*(Are you seriously sleeping right now, Dahl? It's your birthday!)*...I dozed off."

Dahlia looked out the window. The sun was setting.

"What time is it?...*(It's almost six thirty. You must've slept your day away)*...You could say that. What's up?...*(Come to Broken Beach! There's food, music, and great company. Let's have some fun, Dahl! It's your birthday!)*"

Dahlia chuckled and said, "Yeah, that sounds great. When?"

"*(I can pick you up in ten minutes unless you need more time)*...I'll see you in ten."

Dahlia hung up and found a pair of jeans and a long sleeved dark green shirt to wear. She fixed her hair and make-up, brushed her teeth, slipped on her sneakers, and went downstairs to wait for Nina.

Ronan approached the front door of his home. Before he opened the door, a distinct scent filled his nostrils. His eyes changed to jet black in color, and he entered cautiously. The house was eerily quiet.

"Rosie?" Ronan called out. No sound or movement. The smell of blood was strong, and Ronan's stomach tightened. The scent grew more powerful when he entered the living room. That's when he saw it: the pile of bloody body parts on the coffee table. Ronan could feel the blood rushing to his head, and he closed his eyes for a moment.

A piece of paper was pinned to the caretaker's right leg and Ronan removed it to read:

> HOW DOES IT FEEL KNOWING YOU CAN'T SAVE BOTH OF THE WOMEN YOU LOVE?
> ALL IS CRUMBLING AND I'LL WATCH YOU FALL.
> L.R

Ronan crumbled the paper and bared his extended canines. He took out his phone and dialed Eve's number.

(*"Ronan?"*)…Where's Dahlia?…*(She's at Broken Beach with the others, why? What's happened?)*…Rosie's dead. Lucas's making his move. I'm on my way to the beach now…*(You won't make it, Ronan. He's two steps ahead of you.).*"

Ronan didn't reply and hung up.

28. BROKEN BEACH

Eve was right – Dahlia's friends didn't forget. The set up on the beach was for her. A variety of food was laid out on a large blanket with room for people to sit. Music was blaring, everyone was conversing, Nina lit the candles on the small beautifully decorated birthday cake, and 'Happy Birthday' was sung to celebrate a milestone.

Dahlia was sitting on the large beach blanket Nina brought. Tiki torches were set up for light and Dahlia was picking at the cake her friends got her. Reid and Nina were off cozying up to one another by the waves, while Trent watched Lily use her power to manipulate the ocean water into different shapes. Dahlia tried not to look at Carter who wouldn't take his eyes off of her.

"I'm not going to disappear if you stop looking at me" Dahlia told him.

"How do you know?" he asked.

Dahlia looked at him and he smirked.

"Hilarious." She gave him the same smirk.

"That's not why I'm looking at you, although that's a concern we all have tonight," Carter said to Dahlia.

"Then why are you?"

"I'm trying to figure out why you're so nervous around me."

"It could be the fact that I'm nervous in general that I might not live to enjoy eighteen, Carter. Not everything has to do with you."

"You're *always* like this around me. I can decipher the difference between certain nervousness."

"Is that right?"

Carter nodded.

Dahlia sighed. "I worry about our friendship, Carter."

Carter furrowed his brow. "Why?"

"Because of Ronan and me. I don't want you to push away from me because of how close I am with him."

"I'm not going to push away from you because of the vampire."

"You already have! Did you forget that little confrontation in the art room?"

"That was resolved, Dahlia. I got upset because I have feelings for you. Any guy who cares about a girl he can't have is going to get angry. Women are the same way, are they not?"

"They are. I just don't like upsetting you. I feel guilty."

"You shouldn't feel guilty at all. I can be difficult, but I know how I feel. If he's who you want to be with, then I can't make you change your mind."

That didn't make Dahlia feel any less guilty.

"I appreciate that, and I know Ronan does, too" Dahlia told him. She stood up and stretched her legs. "I need to walk off this cake."

She held her hand out to Carter as an invitation to walk with her. He stood up and they took a few steps before Dahlia stopped. The others noticed, and when they asked her what was wrong, Dahlia didn't answer.

"Dahlia?" Carter asked.

Dahlia's focus was on the woods she couldn't stop looking into.

"Dahlia?" Carter asked again.

A light started to illuminate a short distance away. Carter was able to make out a figure behind it.

"Dahlia! We have to go!" he shouted.

"Dahlia!" another voice yelled. Dahlia's head turned to the left and she saw Ronan running across the sand.

"Ro-"

Dahlia's eyes closed and she fell upon the sand. The white light metastasized and in that instant Dahlia was gone. All Ronan could hear was a villainous chuckle.

29. VISIBLE DARKNESS

"Where did she go?" Nina asked as everyone gathered together.

"I have a pretty good idea where she went. You need to get Eve and get over to the Rath house" Ronan told the group.

"You think that's where Lucas took her?" asked Trent.

"It makes sense. That's where it all began" Lily replied.

"And we're wasting time talking about it, so let's go!" Carter barked.

"Are you coming with us?" Ronan was asked by Nina.

"I'll meet you there" he responded and disappeared before Nina could blink.

Dahlia blinked a few times before stirring. She could hear the playing of a piano and she sat up. Dahlia glanced around; the walls were badly burned, and she instantly knew where she was.

Dahlia stood up and swayed slightly. She caught her balance and followed the music into the next room. The man on the keys looked at her and stopped playing. He smiled.

"I know you," she said as she squinted her eyes.

"No, you don't. You've only seen me around Seattle" Lucas replied. He stood up from the piano and stepped in front of it.

Dahlia stared at him. He had very sharp features like that of a male model. He had short brown hair and ice blue eyes; now Dahlia knew who she inherited her eye color from.

"By now you know who I am and why I'm here" he stated.

"You want my power, and the only way you can have it is by killing me, right, Dad?"

"Very good. You've done your research, but I see that your friends and grandmother haven't given you the detailed version."

"No, but I'm sure you'll oblige" Dahlia answered. She was staring him down hard and Lucas was intrigued.

"I'd be happy to. It's quite simple, Dahlia. I drain your blood and then say a chant I discovered before you were born with *your* amulet. Malachite is a very powerful stone, and it will get me what I need."

"It's all about you, isn't it? Have you *ever* thought of anybody else other than yourself?"

The question caused Lucas to furrow his brow. "Of course I've thought of others."

"What happened then? One minute you're in love with my mom, and you were happy. You were her best friend. You had a child together! Then all of a sudden you're trying to kill us!"

Lucas was amused. "Ronan told you his theory. I can't disagree with it. I did love Diana, and if she could've only understood, then I wouldn't have had to kill her," he said nonchalantly.

Dahlia's jaw tightened.

"How do you know he told me his theory?"

Lucas smiled. "I know everything you do, Dahlia. I know more about you than you do. I've watched you since you were a child. Your mother couldn't keep you from me. I kept my distance, though. I realized that your power would be more useful to me when it was fully matured."

"Father of the year. You deserve a cookie."

Lucas chuckled. "My dear, I never wanted to be a father. I knew that with both my and Diana's abilities, our child would possess incredible power, and I was right. As soon as I witnessed you resurrect that animal at the carnival, I knew you were just about to your potential."

"That's nice. It's too bad that Ronan interfered eighteen years ago, huh? You wouldn't have had to go through all the trouble of stalking me and killing my mom," Dahlia spat at Lucas.

Lucas's grin grew deadly. "Diana was dead before you woke up. If your little boyfriend didn't show up-"

"I'd be dead right now!" she yelled at him.

"No, not yet you wouldn't be. Instead of having to sneak around trying to find answers, I would've told you anything you wanted to know. I'm not like Eve. I have no interest in protecting you. I only have interest in protecting your power."

"Too bad others don't feel the same as you. You may have a better shot at killing me."

Lucas laughed. "You have a great sense of humor even in your current position. It's cute that you think you can beat me. Fighting will only make it more painful."

"You should be grateful you're even alive today, Lucas."

"Your mother said the same thing. I didn't ask to be saved, Dahlia. That was Diana's doing! But now, I'm the best of both worlds." His smile was from ear to ear. It was terrifying and menacing.

"I would've let you die" Dahlia told her father with a newfound courage. Lucas's smile disappeared and he threw his arm out toward her. Dahlia fell to her knees as she held her head in her hands. She screamed out in pain as Lucas stood over her.

"Is that any way to talk to your father?" he asked when he retracted his arm.

Dahlia regained her posture, wincing. "You're not my father. You're a monster, and I'll take you down."

Lucas snarled at her and zapped her, sending Dahlia across the room. She hit the wall and fell to the ground.

"*That's enough, Lucas!*"

The voice was like thunder cutting through the house. Lucas looked around to see who spoke, and even Dahlia wondered who was there with them. Then she smiled because she knew without a visual.

30. DARK UNITY

A pair of hands lifted Dahlia to her feet. She looked over and saw Carter. A wave of relief surged through her.

"Are you okay?" he whispered to her. Dahlia nodded. She noticed that the only person missing was Ronan.

"Where's Ronan?"

"I have no idea. He told us he'd meet us here" Carter replied. He stepped in front of her and kept his eyes on Lucas.

"It looks like the gang's all here. It's nice to see you again, Eve" Lucas greeted his ex-mother-in-law.

"I'd say it's a pleasure, but you're the last person I want to lay my eyes on" Eve replied.

"Oh, come now, that's not very nice. You were like a mother to me." Lucas's grin was sinister.

"You killed my daughter. I want you to drop dead at my feet" Eve spat.

"Now Eve, do you think it's wise to speak to me like that? It's a matter of life and death."

"'I'll talk to you any way I want to, Lucas."

As their confrontation went back and forth, Dahlia quietly moved toward the staircase to go upstairs. The more Eve talked, the less Lucas paid attention to his daughter.

When Dahlia reached the stairs, she cautiously ascended. She heard commotion downstairs and thought she heard someone yell for her to run. Dahlia didn't hesitate to pick up the pace.

Your friends can't save you.

Dahlia could hear her name being shouted and screams of pain that followed. As much as she wanted to help them, Dahlia knew that she had to get out of there.

Leave them alone, Lucas!

You're on your own. They can't help you, Princess. Looks as though your vampire boyfriend is a no show.

Dahlia rushed down the hallway and nearly jumped out of her skin when a large blast shook the house. She ran into her old nursery and looked out the busted window. Her friends and grandmother were scattered about the yard.

"No, no! Get up!" Dahlia shouted. She saw them start to stir and relief rushed over her.

"Are you guys okay?" she added.

"Lucas put a spell on the house! I'm trying to revoke it, but I can't!" Eve exclaimed.

"Keep trying!"

They can't enter the house again. It's just you and me now.

Of course you did, Lucas. Now what?

Make this easy for me, Dahlia. Just give me your power, die quickly, and everything will go smoothly.

Die quickly? I don't think so. If you want to fight, then we'll fight.

Come and get me.

The yelling of her friends caught her attention. They were all screaming for her to get out of the house.

Then she heard it - the sound of footprints coming up the stairs. She had to think fast. She climbed out the window and carefully moved across the trim of the house to a part of the roof she could easily climb up to. Her friends were yelling for her to be careful, but that was making her more uneasy.

Dahlia kept wondering where Ronan was. Why wasn't he trying to help her? She needed him, now more than ever. She needed his strength against Lucas.

She reached the top of the roof and stood up. She was hoping that the roof would cave in so she wouldn't have to die at the hands of her father. Dahlia knew she wouldn't be that lucky.

"Nice of you to join me," a voice said calmly.

Dahlia looked up to see Lucas standing less than fifteen feet away from her.

31. DEADLY ULTIMATUM

"You look proud of yourself" Dahlia told him.

"This is simple. There's no need to run because you will never get away. If you give yourself up to me now, you save your friends and your grandmother. You fight me, I will kill them all and you'll all be happy together wherever it is you end up in the next life. It's your choice."

"If it's a fight you want, then it's a fight you'll get."

Lucas chuckled. "No, no. I don't want you to fight, silly girl! I want you to give up!"

"Dahlia doesn't give up, Lucas" said a voice behind Dahlia. She turned quickly and saw Ronan, and he looked ready to fight. She smiled and looked at Lucas again.

"Oh, good. He showed up." Lucas didn't sound thrilled.

"Of course I did. I made Diana and Dahlia a promise. I tend to keep it."

"How touching. I don't see where that's possible, Ronan."

Ronan took his place next to Dahlia. "Why's that, Lucas?"

Lucas smiled. "You can't beat me. I'm more powerful than you'll ever be."

"You sure about that?"

Ronan's body was lifted into the air, and he writhed in pain. His back began to arc, and his body began to glow a vibrant ice blue color.

"I'm very sure," said Lucas. His smile was ruthless and it scared Dahlia.

"Lucas, stop! You're killing him!" Dahlia shouted.

"That's the point."

"Please! Stop hurting him!"

Lucas's power retracted and Ronan slammed onto the roof of the house. Dahlia helped him to stand up.

"My daughter and the one who turned me…how sweet."

Dahlia glared at him with a hateful stare.

"You have two choices, Dahlia. You surrender to me and save your friends, or I kill everyone in front of you, starting with the one you love the most who's standing right next to you."

"Don't do it, Dahlia! If you give up to him, everything Diana did would've been for nothing! " Ronan exclaimed.

"I can't let him kill all of you! It's me he wants!" Dahlia yelled at him.

"Your friends aren't worth it," said Lucas.

Ronan looked at him. "Yes, they are! You turned your back on them a long time ago! If anyone deserves to be dead, it's you! What kind of father would kill his only child?!"

Lucas outstretched his hand; Ronan started to scream, and Dahlia watched in horror as Ronan's face started to char.

"Stop! Lucas, stop!" she frantically yelled.

"I have no problem killing him! I'll get what I want in the end, but you need to make a choice! It's either you or everyone!"

"Stop hurting him and I'll give you my answer!"

Lucas's power retracted again, and Ronan landed on his back. Dahlia helped him to his feet and wrapped her arms around him.

"You have to get out of here" he told her. Ronan was breathing heavily, and he couldn't stand up straight. A tear ran down Dahlia's cheek as she looked at his burned face.

"Very touching, Dahlia. You're starting to piss me off now. You've seen what happens when I get angry."

Dahlia's jaw clenched and she turned around slowly. She stepped in front of Ronan to shield him from Lucas.

"I refuse to give you anything! If you really wanted to kill everyone, you would've done it already! You're a damned coward!" Dahlia screamed at her father.

"So, you made your choice then?" Lucas's face twisted in anger. Ronan saw the immediate danger that Dahlia was oblivious to. Ronan knew what made him tick, and Dahlia only just met him that day.

"Get out of the way, Dahlia!" Ronan yelled at her.

"I'm not afraid of this jackass!"

The smirk on Lucas's face didn't faze her. A pair of hands threw Dahlia violently to the side, causing her to roll off the roof of the house. Electric blue fire hit Ronan in the chest, and he catapulted off the roof.

"One down," Lucas said calmly.

32. GOLDEN FLAME

Dahlia dangled off the roof by her right arm. Her left arm was dislocated, but she could feel her healing power working slowly. Dahlia could hear her friends screaming her name and to hold on. She looked up and saw Lucas staring at her in amusement.

"It looks like you could use a hand." Lucas grinned.

Dahlia growled at him.

"Cooperate with me and I will help you off the ledge you're about to fall off of."

Dahlia knew the consequences for her actions. She didn't want everyone to die because of her decision to fight back.

"Okay. I'll cooperate with you," she said. She sounded defeated.

"How can I trust you?"

"I'm dangling off a roof, Lucas! I don't have much choice in the matter! If I really wanted to die, I would've let go! Then you'd get nothing! On second thought…"

Dahlia pondered the idea of falling to her death. Why not? Lucas wouldn't get what he wanted, and she'd be gone so Dahlia wouldn't have to see the aftermath of her decision. Then again, Dahlia couldn't stand the thought of what would happen to her friends and grandmother if she ended her life.

An arm extended toward Dahlia, and she didn't hesitate to take it. Lucas brought her up to the roof; she looked more like him than she wanted to acknowledge. He refused to let her out of his grasp.

"It's about time. You know, your mother didn't like to cooperate with me. If she just did what I told her that night, I might have let her live. She was so adamant about keeping you away from me that her life meant nothing to me anymore."

Dahlia's eyes widened and tears started to form as she stared at the monster that was her father. She could feel her sadness turning into rage as her eyes narrowed. Her right arm shot up and Dahlia ripped Lucas's amulet from his neck and threw it off the roof.

"Why would you do that?!" Lucas shouted. His eyes changed from his normal blue to jet black.

"I finally have the strength to," Dahlia said through gritted teeth. With everything she had, with every emotion all burning into one, her arms pushed against Lucas's chest. She saw it;
the gold coming from her hands. Dahlia concentrated as hard as she could, and a large ball of golden flame was sent at Lucas.

Dahlia stepped back; Lucas wailed as the flame caused his skin to burn at an incredible rate. To Dahlia's amazement, it didn't faze her to watch. He killed her mother, he hurt Ronan, he threatened her friends, and he wanted her power for himself. This was justice for her; for him to die the same way Diana did.

When all that remained was his ashes, Dahlia could hear everyone yelling for her to come down.

"Just jump! I got you!" Lily yelled.

"Are you insane?!" Dahlia exclaimed.

"I can control air, remember?! Just do it!"

"Listen to her, Dahlia! She won't let you fall!" Trent added.

Dahlia closed her eyes and jumped like she was told. She felt the wind in her hair, and when her feet touched the ground, she opened her eyes and the wind disappeared.

"Wow" she whispered to herself.

She found Lucas's amulet on the ground and picked it up. Dahlia hurried to her friends and threw her arms around her grandmother.

"Are you guys okay?" she asked frantically.

"We're all fine, dear. We're glad you're okay. I'm going to destroy his amulet once and for all" Eve responded.

Dahlia placed it in her hand. "Please do."

She looked around and noticed someone was missing.

"Where's Ronan?" Dahlia asked her friends.

The group went quiet. Dahlia glanced at everyone individually.

"Guys? Where's Ronan?" she asked again.

"I'm sorry, Dahlia. Ronan's gone" Reid told her sympathetically.

"What are you talking about?"

"Lucas killed him, Dahl, when he hit him with the energy. We tried to-"

"Where is he?!" Dahlia exclaimed.

"There's nothing you can do, Dahlia," said Carter.

"Where is he?!" she screamed.

"He was moved closer to the group of oak trees." Nina pointed in their direction and Dahlia took off running.

"Dahlia!" Carter shouted.

"Let her go. She needs to see for herself" Lily told him.

"That's what I'm worried about" he replied and started walking after her.

33. WAKE THE DEAD

Dahlia found Ronan's lifeless body by the trunk of one of the large oak trees and fell to her knees beside him. His face was badly burned, as well as the area where the energy hit him. Tears began to fall, and she traced her fingers along his jaw line.

Dahlia placed her hands over the wounded area on his chest and began to focus on healing the wound. More tears fell, making her eyesight blurry and making it harder for Dahlia to concentrate.

"Dahlia" she heard someone say behind her.

"He can't be dead. Vampires are already dead. This doesn't make sense."

"He's gone. There's nothing you can do."

"No! I don't believe that! I can bring him back!" she yelled.

"Are you insane? You'll kill yourself!" Carter exclaimed.

The rest of the group joined Carter and watched as Dahlia fell apart in front of them.

"I have to try!"

"Your resurrection power won't work on him. Ronan wasn't technically alive, Dahl. Please don't do this. We almost lost you once!" Nina was practically in tears as she begged her to stop.

"Stop! If this was Reid, you'd do *anything* in your power to save him! I need to try, no matter what happens! I'd appreciate your support because *that's* what I need right now!"

"Go ahead, honey" Eve encouraged her granddaughter.

"Eve!" Carter shouted.

"Don't you raise your voice to me!" she snapped at him.

Dahlia took off her amulet and placed it on Ronan's chest. She cleared her mind of every emotion and every thought not related to Ronan's recovery. As she concentrated, the glow coming from her hands turned to a vibrant purple in color and pain started to rip through her. As much as she wanted to stop, she knew she couldn't. She screamed out in pain, but the wound on his chest was healing and she had to hold on a little longer.

"You have to stop her, Eve! Stop her now!" Reid shouted.

Eve was watching in fascination. She couldn't think, let alone speak. Tears rolled down her cheeks as she watched the purple glow grow larger.

Dahlia slumped over and Carter rushed to her side. Ronan sat up gasping for air. He looked at everyone, then noticed Dahlia beside him unconscious.

"What the hell happened?!" Ronan shouted.

"I don't...believe it. She brought you back," Eve said breathlessly.

"Is she crazy?! Dahlia!"

"She's still breathing!" Carter exclaimed.

"We need to get her home right now!" Ronan stood up and swayed a bit.

"Destroy that amulet first, Eve," said Trent.

Eve nodded, tossed the amulet to the ground, and shot witch flame at it. They all watched it burn to ash before leaving.

Ronan carried Dahlia into the house and immediately went upstairs without a word.

"We should all be here when she wakes up," said Nina as she huddled closer to Reid.

"I think it would be best if you all went on home. You can always see her tomorrow" Eve suggested.

"But-"

"No buts, Nina. The only people who will be here when she wakes is Ronan and me. If all of you bombard her, it may freak her out."

"I just thought-"

"Eve's right, we should all go home and get some sleep. It's been one hell of a day and I doubt Dahlia would want all of us crowding her" Carter interrupted.

Everyone looked at him incredulously.

"You of all people I expected to fight her on this," said Reid.

"I'm done fighting. Besides, Dahlia made her choice and it's about time I respect that."

Carter ignored their stares, kissed Eve on the cheek, and walked back outside. Soon, everybody was doing the same and Eve locked the door once Trent closed it.

34. INTO THE STARS

Dahlia's eyes opened slowly. She was in her own room, and she smiled slightly. She sat up and saw Ronan sitting in her desk chair looking at her. He didn't look happy. She was just happy he was alive.

"Thank god" she breathed with relief.

"You nearly killed yourself."

"That's all you have to say?" Dahlia asked him.

"What do you want me to say?"

"How about a thank you? That's a great start."

"Thank you? You nearly died and you want me to thank you?" His tone was cold.

"What the hell's wrong with you, Ronan?!"

"You shouldn't have saved me."

Dahlia was appalled by his statement. "Are you kidding me? Yes, I should've! And I'd do it again!" she yelled at him.

Ronan abruptly gets to his feet. "Don't you ever say that again! I'd never let you do it a second time! The next time would most definitely kill you! What the hell are you thinking?!"

Dahlia gets to her feet. "I'll say whatever the hell I want to! How do you know it would kill me next time?!"

"Your body could barely handle it this time!"

"That doesn't mean I can't do it again!"

They yelled at each other back and forth. Eve could hear them downstairs, but she made no effort to stop it.

"Just stop, Ronan! Stop! Yelling's getting us nowhere!" Dahlia exclaimed. Ronan sighed and looked at the floor.

"You took the biggest risk with your life. What if you died? It would've been for nothing." He sounded defeated.

"It wasn't for nothing." Dahlia walked up to Ronan and forced him to look at her. "I had to try. Wouldn't you do that for someone you love?"

"Love?" he questioned her.

"Do you think I'd do that for just anyone? I can't imagine living in this world without you in it, and I don't want to. I did it because I love you."

Ronan's hands cupped Dahlia's cheeks. "Are you sure?"

Dahlia smiled. "Don't question me."

Ronan smiled back. "I love you, too." He rested his forehead against hers and Dahlia smiled.

***

It was eight thirty in the evening and eight people were gathered on the shores of Broken Beach. Each person held a white lit paper lantern in their hand. Everyone was dressed, not in the traditional black, but in white to match the lanterns. It was a memorial for Diana.

Everyone was saying a few kind words about the deceased, and Dahlia took all the words in. Tears hadn't begun to fall yet, but she knew they would. Everything being said was beautiful, and Dahlia wasn't sure if she could say something that wouldn't be repeated already.

Ronan squeezed Dahlia's hand when it came to her turn to talk. She was the last to speak.

"How can I top what everyone else has said? This is my second memorial for my mom, and the first time I couldn't speak. It was too painful to. But now, after everything that's happened and everything that I've been told, it's a little easier.

"I understand why my mom didn't want to tell me about who she really was and who my father was. It hurt her, and she wanted to protect me. But she couldn't, and it cost her. She'll never be forgotten, and I don't know anyone who would try to forget her.

"Her death didn't cause just pain. A lot of good came out of it if that makes sense. I was able to connect with the only other blood relative I have. I was able to learn more about myself and the potential I have to be better. I met the most incredible group of people I've ever encountered, and I've even fallen in love.

"Sometimes I think that she knew this would happen. That all of this was already mapped out. I think secretly she wanted to tell me the truth, but it was difficult for her. Not just because of the danger, but because this was a part of her world she walked away from. I was angry with her at first for not telling me and preparing me for what was going to happen, but I know now that I can't be mad. I had all the help and support I could ask for.

"She was the greatest mother-" Dahlia had to pause. The tears had finally begun to fall, and Ronan rubbed her back in condolence.

She began again. "She was the greatest mother I could ever ask for. I wouldn't trade her in for anyone else, and I know that I'll see her again when the time comes. For now, I'll remember all the good and bad memories because that's what I have left of her. I miss her terribly, and if the only way I can see her is in my dreams, I'll take it. I love you, Mom. I always will and nothing will change that."

Dahlia was the first to let her lantern fly, followed by Eve, and then the others. She wiped the tears from her eyes and watched as the lights of the lantern flew further and further away with a sad smile.

Once she hugged everyone, Ronan drew her close and kissed her forehead.

"I can still feel her" Dahlia whispered.

"You always will, love" Ronan replied.

Dahlia smiled and they all made their leave from the beach.

ABOUT THE AUTHOR

A.L. FLAGG IS A 34-YEAR-OLD SINGLE MOM WHO ENJOYS WRITING, DRAWING, SPENDING TIME WITH HER LOVED ONES, AND BEING IN THE GREAT OUTDOORS. SHE LOVES TAKING ROAD TRIPS OUT TO SALEM - ESPECIALLY DURING THE FALL. HER CREATIVITY COMES TO LIFE BEING IN A PLACE SHE LOVES. EVEN THOUGH SHE HAS A BUSY LIFESTYLE WITH RAISING A TINY HUMAN AND GOING TO SCHOOL, SHE STILL MAKES TIME TO DO WHAT SHE LOVES TO DO THE MOST - CREATING WORLD'S THAT PEOPLE CAN ESCAPE TO.

TO KEEP UP WITH MY WORK, CHECK OUT MY WEBSITE:
HTTPS://AUTHORAFLAGG.WIXSITE.COM/WEBSITE

Made in the USA
Coppell, TX
30 June 2022